P9-CDA-675

Bad Apple

Also by Laura Ruby

PLAY ME
GOOD GIRLS

For Younger Readers

THE CHAOS KING
THE WALL AND THE WING
LILY'S GHOSTS

Bad Apple

LAURA RUBY

An Imprint of HarperCollinsPublishers

HarperTeen is an imprint of HarperCollins Publishers.

Bad Apple

Copyright © 2009 by Laura Ruby
www.harperteen.com

Library of Congress Cataloging-in-Publication Data
Ruby, Laura.
Bad apple / Laura Ruby. — 1st ed.
    p. cm.
Summary: Tola Riley, a high school junior, struggles to
tell the truth when she and her art teacher are accused of
having an affair.
    ISBN 978-0-06-124330-1
    [1. Teacher-student relationships—Fiction.
2. Cyberbullying—Fiction. 3. High schools—Fiction.
4. Schools—Fiction. 5. Family problems—Fiction.
6. Divorce—Fiction.] I. Title.
PZ7.R83138Bad 2009   2009001409
[Fic]—dc22   CIP
                                                 AC

Typography by Ray Shappell
10 11 12 13   LP/RRDB   10 9 8 7 6 5 4 3 2

First Edition

For Ray of Sunshine
Shine on

The way to read a fairy tale is to throw yourself in.

—*W. H. Auden*

All children are artists. The problem is how to remain an artist once he grows up.

—*Pablo Picasso*

THE FUTURE IS GRIMM

Mr. Mymer, my art teacher, is tall and skinny with floppy hair the color of yams and a peculiar affection for "funny" T-shirts: CLUB SANDWICHES, NOT SEALS. YOGA IS FOR POSERS. FULL FRONTAL NERDITY. When my mother met him at parent-teacher conferences, she said he seemed like a very interesting person. She doesn't say that anymore. Now she says things like he's "evil," "a criminal," and "a predator."

After she says these things, she sometimes stares at me as if I'm a wounded bird flapping around her living room—maybe something you want to help, maybe something you want to smack with a broom. She opens and closes her mouth as if she might call *me* a name, too, but she never does.

I think the name is "liar."

My father didn't go to the parent-teacher conferences. He was on his honeymoon. His new wife is Hannalore, which is

German for *I keep poisoned apples in my purse.*

"No, stupid," says my sister, Tiffany. "It's German for *I haul spoiled stepchildren into the woods and leave them for the wolves. I gather the bones that are left and crush them to a powder. I drink the powder in my afternoon tea. It keeps my skin looking young.*"

Hannalore is six hundred feet tall and looks like one of those opera singers. You know the ones. They wear the metal breastplates and the big hats with the horns. They're always the last to sing.

Like Hannalore, the Brothers Grimm also came from Germany. We all know what kind of tales the brothers had to tell. Bad things have gone down in Germany.

"You're such an idiot, Tola," says my sister, her eyes narrow as punctures. "Ever hear of the Spanish Inquisition? The Salem witch trials? *Slavery?* Bad stuff goes down everywhere."

But my sister doesn't really care about the Brothers Grimm or anything else. After a few minutes of talking about it, she suddenly shrieks: "Shut up! Shut up about the Brothers Grimm! Why does everything you say have some sort of literary reference? Why do you carry around that stupid book? How pretentious are you?"

Someone who wears lavender contact lenses shouldn't talk about being pretentious. I refuse to call my sister Tiffany, so I call her Madge. Madge is eighteen going on Crypt Keeper and cries all the time. I often find her curled up on her bed, wailing like a lost kitten. When you ask her what's wrong, she can never explain. "Life," she says. Or, more specifically, "Everything." Sometimes she hyperventilates. She carries around a supply of brown lunch bags just in case she has to sit and breathe into one.

Only people named Madge breathe into brown lunch bags.

Madge has been to four doctors—one regular one and three therapists. She doesn't like therapists. She calls them voodoo headshrinker freaks. She says that all they want to do is blame our parents for her problems when it's the whole world that's in pain.

I myself have not been to any therapists, which is funny, considering that my sister is (was?) the golden girl and I'm the bad seed. Five years ago, at one of the parent-teacher conferences my mother enjoys so much, my sixth-grade math teacher told my mother that though I was doing better in class, I still stared out the window and appeared stupid. Those were her exact words, too. "She still stares out the window and appears stupid." This is not the sort of thing you say to my mother about one of her children. My mother used her coldest voice—the voice so arctic and furious that icicles spiked the air as she spoke—to tell off my teacher. It took a while. A half hour, maybe. (I'm not sure how long because I was staring out the window and appearing stupid.) My teacher got paler and paler as my mother told her how inappropriate and ridiculous and irresponsible this comment was and how rude and naive and inept the teacher was. My mother talked until the teacher blended in with the white board behind her. And then my mother grabbed my arm and yanked me from the room.

In the car on the way home, my mother used that same freezemonster voice to tell me that I'd better start paying attention in class and living up to my potential, or she would send me to a monastery in Nepal, where I'd spend my life combing fleas from the yaks.

I told my grandpa Joe what my mom said. He patted my hand and declared that he'd never met a yak he didn't like.

Me, Mom, Madge, and the yaks. Sounds bad, but it's not. It wasn't. Take the teachers. Most of them are nice. Sometimes I draw portraits of them and leave the pictures on their desks. That doesn't thrill some of the other kids, who think I'm a brownnoser. But that's not true, either. I like to draw, and the teachers are there just waiting to be drawn. Besides, the things I draw aren't *always* the kinds of things that teachers find flattering. Like, say, putting Ms. Rothschild's head on a rabbit's body. Or drawing Mr. Anderson with a tail. Ms. Rothschild thought her portrait was hilarious; Mr. Anderson, not so much. Actually, that last drawing got me a trip to the principal's office.

The principal: "Is this supposed to be a joke?"

Me: "No, it's a present."

The principal: "A present?"

Me: "As in gift."

The principal (muttering): "You couldn't have given him an apple?"

Me: "You think he would have liked fruit better?"

The principal: "You're a smart girl, so I'm going to be blunt. I think you'd be a lot happier if you stopped acting so weird."

Me: "Who says I'm not happy?"

But maybe he was right, because nobody's happy now.

Before Mr. Mymer, these are the kinds of things that people said about me:

1. In third grade, Tola Riley ate nine funnel cakes at the school carnival and then puked them up on the Tilt-A-Whirl.

2. In fourth grade, Tola Riley stole Chelsea Patrick's American Girl doll—one of those creepy twin dolls—and tried to flush it down the toilet, flooding the school bathroom and causing thousands of dollars' worth of damage.

3. In sixth grade, Tola Riley ran down Josh Beck, the fastest kid in the whole school, so she could rip out a lock of his hair to use in a spell.

4. In eighth grade, Tola Riley drew a picture of one

of her teachers with a noose around his neck and was almost suspended.

5. In ninth grade, Tola Riley was caught making out with Michael Brandeis in the broom closet and was almost suspended.

6. In tenth, Tola Riley was caught making out with June Leon in the girls' room and was almost suspended.

7. In eleventh, Tola Riley was making out with John MacGuire at a party when, for no reason at all, she smashed him in the head with a fishbowl and swallowed the goldfish.

8. She has strange piercings in mysterious places.

9. She's descended from fairies, trolls, munchkins, and/or garden gnomes.

10. She has ADHD, bipolar disorder, Asperger's, and/or psychic powers.

I think this stuff is funny; at least, I used to. No one really believed any of the stories; they just needed something to talk about. Everyone loves a villain. Or maybe not a villain, exactly, but someone you can point out and say, "I might be weird, but I'm not weird like *her*." I was cool with that. I had my friends. I didn't need to be like the rest of the drooling high-school idiots—obsessed with sex, YouTube, MySpace, Facebook, texting, drinking, and UV rays (*Orange is the new tan!*). Let people think I was crazy; let them think I would say anything, draw anything, do anything—what did I care?

Now that I do care, now that I'm trying to tell my own story, no one is listening. Madge says I haven't helped my case by chopping off my hair and dyeing it a shiny emerald green (in addition to the nose ring my mother nearly had a stroke over).

I say, "About a hundred other juniors have dyed hair and pierced body parts. And that's just the guys."

"Congratulations," says Madge. "You're a teenage cliché." She goes back to applying her makeup, or reapplying what she's cried off. "Don't walk too close to me in the mall today, okay? I don't want anyone to know we're related."

"I never made out with Michael Brandeis, you know," I say. "He made that up."

Madge shellacs her bloodless lips with gloss. "Who?"

For the record:
1. I didn't throw up.
2. I buried it under the monkey bars.
3. Hell hath no fury like the boy beaten in the hundred-yard dash.
4. It wasn't a noose; it was a necklace of bones.
5. No.
6. It wasn't the bathroom; it was the art room.
7. The fish was saved.
8. The nose is strange and mysterious enough. Just try to draw one that doesn't come out looking like something that belongs on a grizzly bear.

    9. Fairies, definitely.

    10. I know what you're thinking right now.

You're thinking: *Is* she a liar? Or is she really crazy?

All I can tell you is that I read too many fairy tales about children left to be roasted by hags, vengeful stepsisters so desperate for love they'll cut off their own feet, and girls locked up in towers with only their hair for company.

I didn't know all the tales were true.

(*comments*)

A Willow Park High School art teacher, Albert Mymer, was suspended with pay pending an investigation into an alleged relationship with a sixteen-year-old student.

According to a witness, the teacher and student were observed lunching together at a New York City café. Sources within the school administration say that the witness, a fellow student of the alleged victim, described inappropriate personal contact. She also described an exchange of gifts, including a book. Other witnesses interviewed suggest that this is a pattern of behavior.

"I would like to say I'm shocked," said a coworker of Al Mymer, who wished not to be identified. "But I'm not."

Police and school officials are continuing their investigation.

—*Dana Hudson,* North Jersey Ledger

"Subject was interviewed at her house with mother present. She was cooperative but guarded during interview. Denied allegations of abuse but admitted that she wanted to protect her teacher from punishment."

—*Detective J. Murray*

"She sort of lost it when my—I mean *our*—dad left us, and my mom started treating us like we were in kindergarten. At least, that's what my therapist thinks. If you can trust the opinion of a therapist. Which, mostly, you can't. Therapists are crazy.

"Look, she's always been weird. She was born that way, so it's not like you can blame her—at least not totally. No one asks to be born."

—*Tiffany Riley, sister*

"It's true that I was focused on other things at the time. I admit that. I take full responsibility. Maybe if I'd been around a bit more, none of this would have happened."

—*Richard Riley, father*

"Do you really think that it was just that one time? Give me a break. That skanky little freak is getting exactly what she deserves. Sooner or later, everybody does."

—*Chelsea Patrick, classmate*

SQUIRRELS CAN'T
BE TRUSTED

It's been two weeks since the rumors started, one week since Mr. Mymer was suspended, and four days since my mom had to change our phone numbers. I'm still allowed out of the house, but—ironically—only for school. No clubs. No activities. Except for homework, no computer. And no talking to the reporters who skulk around the house or just outside school grounds. My mother is protecting me until the school-board meeting, where she will attempt to get Mr. Mymer suspended permanently and publicly. Where she will throw me to the wolves.

Mr. Doctor, my mother's husband, drives me back and forth to school. This is okay with me because it is November and damp and cold. Mr. Doctor keeps the radio off, preferring to hum as he drives. He thumps his palms on the steering wheel to the EZ listening music that loops in his head. Despite the cold outside, the windows are cracked.

Mr. Doctor is fond of the word *brisk*. Mr. Doctor should move to Siberia, where brisk is a way of life.

"Can we close the windows?" I say.

"Hmmm?"

"The windows? I'm cold."

"Oh," he says. He presses a button. No windows close, but hot wind shoots from the vents in front of me. My eyeballs start to dry out, then water. Mr. Doctor sees me wiping at my eyes and manages to look both irritated and terrified.

"Don't worry," I say. "I'm not crying."

"Oh. Well." He clears his throat. It is hard for Mr. Doctor to hold conversations like a normal person. "I suppose I wouldn't blame you if you were."

"Nothing happened. I keep telling everyone."

He doesn't say, "Witnesses." He doesn't say, "Investigation." He doesn't say, "Pants on fire."

He says, "Um hmm," in a way that neither agrees nor disagrees. He's Neutral with a capital *N*, that Mr. Doctor. He's our personal Switzerland.

"Why doesn't Mom drive me to school?"

This he doesn't even try to answer. We both know it's a stupid question. Mom makes him drive me and Madge everywhere. (You'd think that Madge would want to drive herself around, but Mom's afraid Madge will have a crippling panic attack and end up in a ditch.) I think that's why Mom married him: his willingness to jump in the car at every opportunity, like a Labrador with a license.

But then that's not the only reason why Mom picked him. There's the money. The security. The teeth. Mr. Doctor is an orthodontist. Half my middle school went to him. *I* went to him. That's where he and my mom met. Both of them lingering in the examination room, discussing the Lost Art of Flossing.

"Most people would have taken me out of school," I say. "Most *mothers* would have."

Mr. Doctor keeps his eyes on the road. "Do you want to be kept home?"

At first, my mom wanted me to scream and cry and make a grand confession. She wanted me to go to therapy. She wanted me to name names so that she had someone to punish. But I wouldn't. I won't.

"No, I don't want to be at home."

"That's what I figured," he says. "Besides, your mother is not most mothers, is she?"

He rolls to a stop in front of the school and pops the lock. He waits until I get inside the building before driving away.

I walk down the hall, feeling the weight of eyes. I've always felt the weight of eyes, but now they're heavier, like I'm wearing a lead dress.

I steer past the trophy case, where dusty trophies trumpet the kind of athletic achievements the school hasn't had in years. A clot of freshmen—you can always spot the freshmen—gape. Faster now, I walk by the main office.

Inside, the secretary glances up and frowns at me. The halls around the office have been freshly painted, a long expanse of white just begging for decoration. What would I hang there? *Who* would I hang there?

Even though I'm on the lookout for enemies, I haven't walked far when someone accosts me, one of the Whitestone twins; I can't tell which one. Her gray eyes glint like rocks at the bottom of a stream as she says, "So. Is he going to leave his wife? Are you guys gonna run off to Mexico or something?"

I say, "Nobody's running anywhere."

"Did he promise to marry you?"

"He didn't do anything."

"That's not what I heard," she says.

I hate people; that's my problem. "The truth is," I say, "he's having my baby. It's a medical miracle. Someone call the newspapers."

"Nice *hair*," she spits. She stomps off, her cheerleader skirt swishing.

I'm not the only one who loves Mr. Mymer.

I make it to my first class without anyone grabbing my backpack and throwing it in a toilet. Madge says I should just drop out since most of my classes are a joke. Which is true. Except for art, I don't take honors classes, I don't take AP. I've always preferred slogging along with the druggies, the perpetually confused, the motivationally impaired. Maybe not a great plan for a girl in my situation. Mr. Lambright, my lit teacher, makes desperate attempts to interest us in words, in meanings. He plays scratchy old records on an ancient record player and has us study the lyrics.

"*Before our eyes, buzzing like flies.* Now, what do you think that means? Anybody? Loren? Jamie? Miles? Miles!"

Miles isn't interested in song lyrics. Miles has spent the entire period pointing at me, performing obscene tongue acrobatics for the entertainment of his friends.

"Miles Rosentople!"

Miles slurps his lizard tongue back in his mouth. "Huh?"

"Is that good or bad?"

"Is what good or bad?"

"The phrase 'buzzing like flies.' Do you think that's a good or a bad thing?"

"I don't know," he says. He licks his lips, still smirking at me. "Good?"

In my next class, Mr. Anderson prepares us, his little biology soldiers, for the arrival of fetal pigs, which we are to dismember for credit. I don't know why we can't get a formaldehyde-free computer program and *pretend* to dissect the pigs. Maybe because Mr. Anderson is almost a million years old, joined the marines when he was six, and believes that we're all part of the food chain and always had and always would eat or destroy one another. "Look," Mr. Anderson says, "if you were one of the last humans alive and you were stranded in the Kalahari Desert, do you think that a lion wouldn't eat you if it were hungry? Do you honestly think that one lion would say to another lion, 'Hey, don't eat the naked, defenseless two-leggers, there's only one thousand three hundred and sixty-three left in the world'? Baloney! And that's exactly what these pigs would be if we weren't using them to get you kids interested enough to learn a little science—baloney! And that's life, my friends! Better accept that now!"

As he rants, I slip the copy of *Grimm's Fairy Tales* from my backpack and flip through the pages, reading the notes that my father scribbled in the margins back when he was a frustrated teenager forced to flay unsuspecting frogs: *Good and evil aren't abstract concepts. Always use your magic for good. This class is bogus.*

In history, we have a mock election. When the results are tallied, it turns out that a bunch of us voted for someone we could never in a million years picture as the leader of the free world. We eye each other with suspicion, wondering who the traitors are.

Then, Cooking II. Mrs. Duckmann, aka the Duck, doesn't believe in cooking. She believes in splitting recipes in neat columns of fractions. She believes in measuring accurately using the right instruments—dry ingredients in little beige plastic cups, liquids in the clear glass. But today she's changing things up. Today, says the Duck, we are going to apply what we have learned in our unit "The Egg" to make something basic but essential for many recipes.

"Today," she announces, with all the fanfare of a newscaster announcing the results of the Super Bowl, "we are making mayonnaise."

My partner, a ginormous senior who looks like a Transformer—I imagine his parts swiveling and recombining to change him from a human to an industrial fridge—breaks out in applause.

I raise my hand. "Couldn't we make something more complicated? Like cookies, maybe? Cookies have eggs."

Some of the teachers won't look at me; some of the teachers won't stop staring. The Duck's eyes widen as if surprised to see me sitting in front of her. Her numerous wrinkles fold in origami patterns of concern. She looks like the witch in "Hansel and Gretel" must have looked right before she threw Gretel in the oven.

"If the lesson is upsetting you," she says sweetly, "perhaps you'd like to go to the principal's office?"

The principal is not happy to see me.

Art, finally. Mr. Mymer is gone, but the art room, his room, is still my favorite place to be. I love the smell of paint, of clay and charcoal, the smells of things that make you believe that you will be okay.

I remember walking into the art room as a freshman and gaping at the giant murals on the walls, paintings on easels, sculptures made of wire and Styrofoam.

It was the only class I was looking forward to, even then. My dad was an artist, a sculptor. He made architectural models. Little houses, buildings, office parks, all perfectly scaled down to size. For my sister and me, he made Cinderella's castle, the humble cabin of the Dwarves, Rapunzel's tower. Who needed dolls?

So, that first day of high school, I brought a tiny house I'd built. A crazy off-kilter house, the kind of house some kind of punk fairy would have built for herself. But I didn't know it would be so hard to get the details right. My dad helped me cut the wood and the foam boards. I used clay for the rest. I had tucked it carefully in a brown paper bag so that no one would see it until the Big Unveiling.

Mr. Mymer, the teacher, was not old, not young, and built like one of Van Gogh's sunflowers: big head bobbing on a long, thin stalk. He had a fat nose and a weird black mole begging for surgery on his cheek. He wore black glasses, faded jeans, and some sort of fifties bowling shirt over a T-shirt. The T-shirt said SQUIRRELS CAN'T BE TRUSTED. His eyes were huge and bright and bored right into you.

I decided he was hot.

When the bell rang, he was quiet for so long we thought he was having one of those seizures, you know, the ones where people's brains freeze up, but they look okay from the

outside. Then he said, "I'm supposed to begin by saying art
will free you, that it will transform you, that you will find
yourself remade, renewed, reborn, et cetera, et cetera. And
maybe that will happen for a few of you. But a lot of you will
be bored. And all of you are going to be frustrated. Really
frustrated. You're going to want to tear up your drawings,
trash your sculptures, slash your paintings. I hope you don't.
Because art will reveal your real feelings about the world
better than almost anything else. And who doesn't want to
know their own real feelings about the world? Who doesn't
want to know him or herself?"

He kept talking about what we'd learn and how we'd
learn it. That he would consider us adults and that we didn't
have to ask to use the bathroom or go get a drink of water
(but he also said not to blame him if some random teacher
or administrator caught us in the hall without a pass). That
we would work harder than we've ever worked in any class.
That we should expect to lose a lot of sleep.

I touched the brown paper bag that hid the fairy house. I
already knew myself. And I'd had insomnia since kindergarten. I waited impatiently for him to stop talking. I stared out
the window. I glanced at the clock.

Finally, the bell.

The other kids filed out of the classroom. I brought the
bag up to his desk.

"I have something to show you," I said. Up close, his
eyes were blue enough to hurt.

"And your name is?"

"Tola Riley."

"Okay, Tola. Let's see what you got."

I slipped the fairy house out of the bag and held it out to him like a birthday cake.

My new teacher took the house and examined it from every side. Then he said, "Well."

"It's a house," I said helpfully.

"Yeah, I see that." He peered inside one of the slanted windows. "Any people in here?"

"Who needs people?"

He shrugged. "Right. So, what moved you to build a house?"

"What do you mean?"

"I mean, why a house? Why not a dog? Or a train? Or a train made of dogs?"

I had no idea what he was talking about. I said, "Huh?"

"What were you trying to say with this house?"

Was he being deliberately stupid? "I was just trying to make a cool house."

"Hmmm," he said, nodding. "Okay."

This was not the reaction I'd been going for. "So you don't think artists should build houses. Houses are not worthy."

"Oh no, no! I think it's fine to build houses. There's an old saying about art: 'Practice what you know, and it will help to make clear what you don't know.'"

I frowned so hard my eyebrows ached. "Who said that?"

"I don't know who said it. Rembrandt? Picasso? I can never remember. But it's true. The more you build these little houses, the more you'll realize how much you don't know about little houses. Maybe you don't even like little houses."

"I *love* little houses," I said, taking my own little house and shoving it back in the bag. I wanted to smash it to the ground.

At lunch, I called my dad. "My art teacher is a butthead."

But no, no, he wasn't. And I discovered that I didn't like little houses so much unless my dad made them for me. I started painting instead. I learned that I could fall into a painting and not come out for days. That painting took me to places I never imagined going, like a train made of dogs.

(*comments*)

"I don't like to make statements during ongoing investigations regarding our teachers or our students, but rest assured that we're taking this matter very seriously. We're cooperating with the police; we're cooperating with the victim's family. Our school is an open book. We have nothing whatsoever to hide. That said, any reporter found on school grounds will be prosecuted to the fullest extent of the law."

—*Mr. Thomas Zwieback, principal*

"She might be okay if she'd lose the green hair. What is that supposed to be? Mold?"

—*Miles Rosentople, classmate*

"OMG! That girl is a complete freak. Like a cross between Dracula's ugly little sister and, I don't know, a hobbit. I can't believe anyone in the universe would risk his job for her. I mean, a lot of girls at our school are so much hotter."

—*Heather Whitestone, classmate*

"I wouldn't say she was a liar. More like a storyteller. Always going on about Cinderella and Snow White and whoever. Ask her who dyed the cat blue, and she'd tell you that the fairies did it. Ask her who ate all the cookie dough and threw up behind he couch, and she'd tell you some crap about dwarves. I think that's what drove my mom so nuts, all the dumb little stories. Sometimes you just wanted to scream, will you *please* tell the truth?"

—*Tiffany Riley, sister*

ACHTUNG

Without Mr. Mymer, art is Subs-R-Us. Today, a huge blond woman minces into the art room like one of the dancing hippos from *Fantasia*. Her thick hair is cut in a severe bob that makes her head look like an equilateral triangle. She's as short as she is wide. She looks like Rumpelstiltskin. If Rumpelstiltskin had a cut-rate sex-change operation in a third-world country.

Some subs like to sit at the desk and file their nails. Some read thrillers or text their friends. This one has had Significant Art Training, or so she tells us. As we work on assignments given to us by Mr. Mymer weeks ago, she strolls around the room and inspects the pieces hanging on the walls. "I can see we have lots of talent in this school." She taps a painting. "Look at the influence of Jackson Pollock here, the movement and the texture. Very effective." Effective? Valerie Schenke spilled some paint across her canvas and didn't feel like starting again.

"And this," she says, gesturing at a pseudo-Picasso, which looks like a crime-scene photo. "I'm just amazed at the emotion I see in the woman's face, the sadness." I'm not sure how she can detect the sadness. In the painting, one of the woman's eyes is actually a breast.

She keeps moving alongside the row of paintings until she stops in front of one of mine. I'd painted a woman seated in an empty stone room. The stones around her form a gray mosaic, but her dress is arterial red, and her hair is a thick braid of gold coiled on the floor. A black kitten crouches in her lap, jewel eyes winking. A small window in the corner shows the vast fields and bright sun outside. In the stone over her head, I did something I always do. I painted the title of the piece: *Rapunzel Gets a Cat*. Mr. Mymer said I was really starting to get somewhere.

"Now this," she says, "this one is tricky. I don't know. The concept is interesting, but I don't think it's working as well as it could. The colors are jarring and the composition feels a little off."

Jarring? Off? *What?!* I can feel the hinge of my jaw release and my mouth drop open, like I'm a snake about to wrap my scaly lips around one of those thousand-year-old eggs— black around the edges and green in the middle—that they serve to crazy foodies in Chinatown.

But she's not done. "I'm not really sure what the purpose of the text is. Text can work with art, of course, but you don't want to reduce your art or dumb it down trying to be funny."

Who's *trying*?

And then she drops the ax. It's huge and sharp and likes to chop things, like hope and dreams and pride and dignity. *Chop, chop, chop, chop.*

"See," Rumpelstiltskin says, "how it dies on the canvas?"

Dies, dies, dies, dies. This is what I'm thinking as I walk back to my locker. I hear Chelsea Patrick before I see her and, more importantly, before she sees me. The loud mocking voice, the Gestapo stomp of her boots. I duck into my health class, wondering where I left my nerve.

In class, Ms. Rothschild has us practicing CPR on an armless, legless mannequin named Little Jane™. The boys try to stick their tongues down her sad, plastic throat.

At lunch, June meets me at our usual spot in the cafeteria. She is texting rapidly on her cell phone, which isn't a phone as much as it's some sort of superintelligent NASA communication device with a talent for calling other phones by itself when June isn't using it.

"Speak to aliens yet?" I say.

"Yeah," she says. "You."

June is a lot taller than I am (which is not saying much; if I were a mere two inches shorter I would be legally required to use a child-safety seat in cars). She wears slouchy boy jeans, a gray T-shirt, and blue cat's-eye glasses from a thrift store. We met in the third grade. Scratch that; our moms met when June and I were in third grade, and then our moms arranged a lot of play dates for us mostly so that they could hang out. But as soon as we got into junior high, I saw June less and less. Her mom was obsessed with June's college applications, so she filled up every minute of every day with some kind of activity. Just last year, June had Chinese, viola lessons, soccer, and a summer community-college class called "Whiteness: The Other Side of Racism."

June's my closest friend; she's my only friend. Back when I was stewing in middle-school misery, I thought high school would be different. I thought I'd have a whole bunch of friends, friends like in the books I read, where girls cry together and hug each other and have Big Moments of Sharing and Caring in the girls' room. In our girls' rooms, the girls pee on the toilet seats and scrawl horrible messages about other girls on the walls.

"You know," says June, pulling a sandwich from a brown bag, "we could be wearing uniforms soon, like the Catholic school kids."

I'm already halfway through my sandwich, peanut butter and banana. "Who said that?"

June ignores her own sandwich, her thumbs flying across the keyboard. "I don't know. Someone just sent me a text about it. Would somebody please explain to me why schools would make the girls wear skirts so short that you can see their underwear? How does exposing the thighs of young girls promote good education? Aren't we distracted enough?"

A wadded piece of paper smacks her in the forehead. She slips the NASA phone into her pocket (where it will likely call around for a pizza), uncrumples the note, and holds it up so I can see:

SHOW US YOUR BOOBS!

"They want me to take a photo and send it to their phones."

"Some girls actually do it."

"I know," she says. "Because it's *so* romantic to have absolutely no self-respect."

"And they would just send the picture around to the entire school," I say. "Why not just come to class naked and save everyone the trouble?"

June laughs, flutters her eyelashes, and presses the note to her cheek.

When she does this, there are whoops and hoots of approval from the guys at the next table over—Pete Santorini, Ben Grossman, and Alex Nobody-Can-Pronounce-His-Last-Name. Thing is, they don't whoop and hoot in a mean way, not really. It's their way of flirting or something.

Pete Santorini, Ben Grossman, and Alex Nobody-Can-Pronounce-His-Last-Name then proceed to whoop and hoot at me. In a mean way.

June can tell the difference. "Maybe if you could just explain."

I have explained. Over and over. Nothing happened with Mr. Mymer, at least not the way people think. That I know who the "witness" is; that to her, I'm just another game. But nobody cares. Not June, who is back to texting who-knows-who on her stupid phone. Not even my own mother.

But if I were to explain again, I would blame Georges and Gustav.

In other words, it's the artists' fault. It's always the artists' fault.

First, Georges. As in Georges-Pierre Seurat. French painter, born December 2, 1859, died just thirty-one years later from "meningitis, pneumonia, angina, and/or diphtheria," according to the little pamphlet I picked up at the Museum of Modern Art in the city. Two weeks ago, when life was only the normal kind of horrible, and not the horrible kind of horrible, I went to the Georges Seurat exhibit. It was an exhibit of his drawings, most done in black Conté crayon, which is like regular crayon, only better. The drawings were packed with lots of crazy scribbles, cross-hatchings, and little dots that made them look sort of dreamlike, as if Seurat saw the world through a veil of stars.

He liked to draw actresses and circus performers. Also cows. I looked at the cows a long time. Who knew I liked cows so much? But then, that's what an artist can do. Make you think about cows, even if you weren't planning on it.

I said as much on my blog, the one the lawyer made me take down. But no one seemed to get it. (Several comments said, "You're the cow!") They didn't want to know about farm animals. They wanted to know why we picked a museum and not a motel.

Anyway, after the cows, I went to the museum café and sat in a deserted corner. I took out my favorite journal, the one with the peeved Little Red Riding Hood on the cover, and tried to do what I was supposed to do: write an entry about the exhibit. Instead, though, I sat there, scratching the paper with my pencil, wondering how I could get a shadow to look as dense and velvety as Seurat could, how the mere absence of crayon on the page could burn so hot and white.

I must have been sitting for a long time, scratching at the same spot with my pencil, because when I remembered where I was, an hour had passed, and I was beyond starving. I went up to the counter and ordered a hot chocolate and a dessert plate, which cost about as much as a boob job, and sat back down. I was trying to come up with something brilliant to put in my journal, something about how Seurat was able to elevate a simple cow to the Ethereal Essence of All Cow-ness, when someone cleared his throat. I looked up to see Mr. Mymer standing there, a study in browns and oranges, his pumpkin-colored hair sticking up in every direction, a book—*The World of Gustav Klimt*—under his arm. His T-shirt said: SILENCE IS GOLDEN, DUCT TAPE IS SILVER.

Now that I'm thinking about it, if it weren't for Georges and his stupid cows, I probably would have been on the bus on my way home by the time Mr. Mymer showed up with his stupid T-shirt and his stupid, stupid book. And then what would people be talking about?

June's sandwich still sits uneaten in front of her. I rip off a corner and pop it into my mouth. Cheese.

"Hey!" she says.

"You never eat your food," I say.

"And you can't *stop* eating."

"What's your point?"

I say this last bit loudly, to drown out the jeering of Pete Santorini, Ben Grossman, and Alex Nobody-Can-Pronounce-His-Last-Name.

"Ignore them," June says.

"Yeah?" I say. "How?"

"Okay. Don't ignore them. Distract them."

"With what?"

"With a real boyfriend."

"Right. And who would that be?"

"How about Seven?"

I glance up to see him, a tall bony guy, loping by, his Sideshow Bob curls bobbing. He's carrying a pretzel decorated with ribbons of mustard.

"He grew out his hair," June says. "He looks amazing."

"He looks like a giant caramel with some carpet lint stuck to the top of it."

"Don't you have a crush on him?"

"When I was in the sixth grade."

"You always remember your first love," June says.

I say, "Love schmove."

Is that his real name? And if not, what's the Seven stand for? No one knows. Every year, the first day of school, before the bell rings, before the teacher can call attendance, Seven whispers in his/her ear. So when roll is taken, and all the Jonathans (Jon), Elijahs (Eli), Rogers (T-Ball), and Lucianas (Lulu) have waved off their given names and offered up a nickname they can tolerate, Seven is only and forever Seven.

We ask ourselves, one another, what's it mean? Is it a numerology thing, a religious thing? June wonders if it's a black thing. She polls the other black students in the junior class. They are amused. They begin calling each other Thirty-three, Ninety-two, Decimal Point.

"Infinity, my man, what up?"

"Not much, Pi."

Says June, "Okay, okay, I get it. It was a stupid poll."

"Whiteness," I say. "It's the other side of racism."

"And *you* can just shut up."

Talk about distraction. I'm mesmerized by Seven the Lint-Topped Caramel. I wonder which paint colors I'd have to mix to capture his skin, and how many. White, umber—raw and burnt—sienna, a single drop of crimson like a jewel of blood.

As if he can hear my thoughts, Seven whips his head around and fixes me with a gaze. I freeze, imprisoned in my own body like a princess in the thrall of a spell.

(comments)

"I only spent three days in the classroom, so it isn't as if I know the girl, or have any idea what really happened. I can tell you, however, that she did *not* take well to criticism. She seemed to be under the impression that she was some sort of artistic genius. And she's not the only one. I blame the parents. Too many of them spoiling their little darlings rotten, telling them they can do no wrong. We're raising a generation of lazy brats with an oversized sense of entitlement. What's going to happen when the brats turn thirty and are still living in their mommies' basements?"

—*Belinda Stumpf, substitute teacher*

"The first time I saw her, it was the sixth grade. I was the new kid. She was the first person to say hi to me in the hallway. She was the shortest person in the class, probably in the whole school. I told my mom that there was a girl who was so small she could fit in my pocket. Like Thumbelina or something.

"She's still small, and I still want to put her in my pocket."

—Seven Chillman, classmate

"So, we were 'friends' once a thousand years ago. My mom made her lemonade. So what? What do you think that means? We were friends before we knew who we were. And then we found out."

—Chelsea Patrick, classmate

HAIRBALL

Mr. Doctor picks me up from school and deposits me at home with the usual warnings to go nowhere and speak to no one. He drives back to his office to rescue more children from their own wandering teeth.

I go to my room. My bedroom isn't on the second floor like other bedrooms. It's a third-floor attic room half pasted like an afterthought on the back of the house. It has huge windows on three sides and skylights hacked into the slanted ceiling. The only way to get there is a staircase so steep and narrow that your feet don't fit on the steps, and you have to climb sideways.

Before he left, this room was my father's office. One night right after, when I couldn't sleep, I went up there to think. There wasn't much in the room, a few pens and pencils strewn among the dust bunnies. A couple of storybooks that my dad didn't want piled on the built-in shelves, one of them the old,

marked-up copy of *Grimm's*. In the corner of the room, a
white half-finished model of something, I didn't know what.
Someone's dream home that would never be built.

When I was little, I couldn't go to sleep unless I'd said
good night to Rapunzel's miniature tower and the dwarves'
tiny cabin and listened to my father tell me a story. That night,
on the floor of my father's almost-empty office, I thought
about the fairy tales, how they were basically the stories of
screwed-up families: Stepmother hates gorgeous stepdaugh-
ter, wishes her dead. Father dies and leaves two older sons
with the money and his youngest son with nothing but a
cat. Father lets his crazy wife talk him into leaving his kids
to die in the woods. You could read this kind of stuff in the
newspapers, I thought, except fairy tales were jazzed up with
gnomes and fairies, fancy outfits and happy endings.

The newspapers weren't much on the happy endings.

I couldn't bear what was left in the room, or what wasn't
left, so I sat under the skylight and looked straight up. A full
moon was centered perfectly in the skylight like a gift. I
stared at it until it burned itself into my eyes. Everywhere I
looked, there it was. So, a trade-off: the moon for my father.
Seemed magical enough.

The next morning, my mom found me sleeping on the
bare floor in a wad of blankets. She didn't complain, so I
stayed. My easel is set up right in front of the windows,
directly under the skylight.

● ● ●

But the moon is hours away and I can't paint now, not with the substitute teacher's voice grinding in my head. And I refuse to do any other kind of homework out of principle. I go to the backyard and call for my cat, Pib. We've got a huge yard, six-foot cedar fences on the sides, a thick wall of trees at the back. Perfect for keeping out reporters. I hear the rustling first, then see Pib slinking through the wet leaves. He sidles up to me, but as soon as I reach down to pet him, he bounds away, making for his favorite tree. It's a crazy old oak, with rough whorls of bark bunching around its base like a rumpled nightgown, and a deep black hole hunkering under twisted roots. The bark whines as Pib's claws sink into it. Sometimes Pib just hangs there, stapled to the brown trunk, looking over his shoulder, daring me to catch him.

I turn from the tree and pretend I'm not interested in him anymore. Behind me, I hear the scraping sounds of his claws as he backs down the tree. I wait a few more seconds till he's creeping up behind me, then I turn to grab him. Too slow. He takes off again, racing up the side of the tree, striped lemur tail lashing the air. He meows and then keeps his mouth open so that he seems to be grinning. He could play this game all day.

Even with Pib, I'm *It*.

"Hey, Tola," a voice says.

Mr. Rosentople's dark head pops up like a hairy jack-in-the-box over the fence. I can't see the rest of him, but I know that he's standing on top of a stack of stones he piled on his side of the fence just for this reason. All the better to see you.

I want to say, How's your delinquent son, Miles? When do you think he'll end up in jail? Or maybe, How's the recluse wife? Did you bury her in the basement?

I settle for: "Hey, Mr. R. How are you?"

"He left us a prize again," Mr. Rosentople says.

"Who did?" I know who, and I know the prize, but I don't like talking to Mr. Rosentople. I don't like looking at his stupid hairy face. He has handlebar *eyebrows*.

"Your cat left a mouse on our doorstep."

"Oh," I say.

"At least, I think it was a mouse."

"Right," I say.

"Hard to tell what the things are when your cat gets through with them."

"Uh-huh," I say.

"It really upsets my wife, you know."

"I'm sorry."

"You might think about getting him declawed."

We've had this conversation before, Mr. Rosentople and I. Most adults want to talk about my delicate psyche or my poor poor mother or about the nosy reporters calling day and night, getting into everybody's business. They want to see if they can get the real story out of me. Mr. Rosentople wants to talk about my cat. He's a man obsessed. "I can't get him declawed. Those are his weapons, his protection. He'd be defenseless without them. What if he were attacked by another cat?"

Mr. Rosentople snorts. "Your cat has probably already eaten all the other cats around here."

"I don't think that's fair."

"He's bigger than my dog."

"You have a tiny dog."

"I have a normal dog. Your cat is a beast."

"He's just a cat."

"Why doesn't he leave the mice on *your* doorstep?" says Mr. Rosentople.

"I don't know why," I say. But I'm pretty sure Pib doesn't leave bloody gifts on my doorstep because he doesn't want to upset me. (I love cats, but I also love rabbits and chipmunks and squirrels, oh my.) And I'm pretty sure Pib leaves his kill on Mr. Rosentople's doorstep because Mr. Rosentople is the butcher who wants Pib's claws ripped out. Pib is not stupid. Pib believes in making a statement.

Mr. Rosentople says, "If he doesn't stop doing it, I'm going to have to talk to your mother again."

"You don't need to talk to my mother," I say.

"I'll have to."

"She's just going to tell you the same thing."

"Your mother's a reasonable woman," he says, which proves that he doesn't know the first thing about my mother.

"I'll try to keep a better eye on Pib," I say. "I'll keep him inside more."

"Thank you," says Mr. Rosentople. "That's all I ask."

It's not. But like everyone else, we pretend.

I play Pib's game a while longer, then coax him inside, away from the barbarians who would do him harm.

And, in the kitchen, run smack into another barbarian who would do him harm.

"Get that rabid thing away from me," says Madge, kicking at him with one stocking foot. In the face of her ferocious rage, Pib yawns.

"I wouldn't do that," I say. "He'll bite off your leg and leave it at Mr. Rosentople's."

"Oh, *him*," says Madge. She makes the pronoun sound like a swear. "I can't stand *him*."

"Who can?"

"Mrs. Rosentople, I guess," Madge says. She's emptied all the cookies from a package of Oreos. She wets her finger and presses it inside the bag to get it covered with crumbs. Then she licks her finger. I can tell she hasn't left her bedroom all day. She's wearing her pajama bottoms, and her greasy hair is plastered to her head. On the table is her laptop, which is currently showing *The Pianist*, one of Madge's Top Ten War Films Guaranteed to Depress You into a Coma.

"How about a shower?" I say.

"I'm conserving our natural resources."

"For how long?"

"I'm not taking a shower until Mom cans my stupid therapist."

I had to go see her therapist once for a family session. I didn't think he was so bad. "Why? He seemed nice enough," I say.

"Nice? *Nice?*" she says. "Please. They all start out that way, until they try to convince you to take drugs." Madge's skin is the gray of skim milk, and her eyes look like she's used red liner on them. If I ever wanted to paint a ghoul, I've got the ideal model. Maybe drugs could stop the transformation before it is complete.

I say, "Don't some people need drugs?"

"Do you want to know what the latest research says? That drugs don't work. That they're no better than placebos. And some other studies say that the drugs can increase thoughts of suicide in anyone under eighteen. The drug companies don't want you to know that you're paying three hundred dollars a month to take something that's just as effective as a sugar pill or will make you want to kill yourself."

"Do the drugs really cost three hundred a month?"

"That's not the point!" she yells. "Why don't you ever listen?"

Sometimes I think that Madge is like one of those stepsisters, never happy with anything. Like she's going to make me dress in rags and sweep out the fireplace. "I'm listening, I'm listening."

"Therapists just like to hang out with crazy people so they don't feel so bad about themselves."

Madge is feeling bad about herself. She's spent the last month working on her essay for Harvard, even though she doesn't even want to go there. I helpfully remind her of this fact.

She sneers. "I still want to get in."

"Why?"

"What do you mean, why? So that I could say I got in."

"Mom says you might get in all your schools if you'd only finish the essays and submit the applications."

She's mad again. "So?"

"So . . . okay. I see what you mean," I say, even though I absolutely don't. Madge is supposed to be away at school. This time last year, she had all her applications and essays ready, all she had to do was press Send. Then our high school announced that every senior with a grade point average over 4.0 would be considered valedictorian of the class, which meant that there would be more than forty-plus valedictorians jostling for space at graduation. Madge raged for three days. After that, she made her own announcement: She would be putting college on hold so that she could do a "gap" year. I thought that gap years were for joining the Peace Corps. Apparently, they're for watching war movies, breathing into bags, and declaring moratoriums on bathing.

"Anyway," Madge says, "how do you know what Mom says about anything? Is she talking to you now?"

"She's doing that nontalking talking thing."

Madge nods. She knows what I mean. When my mom is mad, she talks about everything but what's really making her mad. Which has the interesting effect of making her sound even madder.

"Instead of talking about the school-board meeting or Mr. Mymer or what the cops said," I tell Madge, "she talks about you and your college applications."

"Uh-huh," says Madge. "She doesn't talk to me about college." Madge doesn't say what they talk about. I bet I can guess.

"Mom thinks I'm a liar," I say.

Madge shrugs. "She thinks we're both full of it."

"But *why?*"

"She's been pissed off ever since I wrote that affidavit for Dad last spring."

"That was six months ago," I say.

"That's Mom for you."

"And *I* didn't write it! I didn't even read it!"

"She probably thinks you agreed with me."

"How can I agree with what you wrote if I don't know what you wrote?"

Madge finishes licking the cookie crumbs out of the Oreo bag and scrapes the cookies back in the package. I make a mental note not to eat any.

"I told you what I wrote," Madge says. "I said I didn't think the court should tell us where we could spend our weekends, and if we wanted to spend them at Dad's, then we should be able to. That if we wanted to live with him, we should be able to. I mean, *duh*, I wrote it for you. I turned eighteen, so I can do whatever I want. You didn't want me to defend your rights?"

"Well, yeah, but . . ."

"So then what are you whining about?"

"I'm not whining," I say.

"By the way, another reporter called."

"How did they get the new number?"

"They're reporters, stupid. It is their job." Madge rummages in the fridge and in the drawers. "I was originally thinking about a hunger strike, but I'm too hungry right now."

"That's genetic," I say.

Madge laughs. Her laughs are more like the shrieks of banshees. When Madge laughs, puppies have nightmares. "I'm hungry because I didn't have breakfast or lunch. You, on the other hand, should wear a sign that says WILL EAT FOR FOOD."

"I'm not sure I know what you mean."

"What else is new?" she says.

She grabs some slices of white bread that she finds in the bread box. She rolls the bread into little rubbery balls that she tosses into her mouth. I like to do this, too, but I put chocolate chips in the center of the bread. In my opinion, it's not worth the effort without the chips.

"You need chips," I say.

"We have chips? Why didn't you tell me that, you bitch?"

This is what passes for conversation with the Riley sisters. Can't you just feel the love?

It wasn't always like this. Once upon a time, there were four of us: one slightly sarcastic mom, one slightly gloomy dad, two girls who only occasionally hated each other. Now we walk around snarking and sniping like some fake movie family.

I think about the affidavit, why she wrote it. Maybe Madge thought Dad would take her with him. Maybe she thought he would save her.

Pib crouches under the kitchen table and hacks up a hairball. He backs away from it as if he's shocked at what's been fermenting inside him.

(*comments*)

"My dad left two years ago. I don't blame him; I would have left, too. I can't imagine having to be married to my mom. She's what you call a nutcracker, okay? And, sure, it affected Tola, just like I said it did. But Tola isn't as close to Dad as I am. She *thinks* she is, but she's not."

—*Tiffany Riley, sister*

"You always feel sorry for a girl like that. A lonely girl. Scared. The green hair is a big clue. But then, students do tell stories to get attention. Girls tell stories. And Mr. Mymer was a convenient target for impressionable girls. I told him not to wear those ridiculous T-shirts. I told him to get a haircut. He laughed and said I worried too much. Now look who's worried."

—*Tamara Duckmann, teacher*

"She has this huge cat. Enormous. I've never seen a cat that big, except in a zoo. It's almost as big as she is. It follows her down the street like a dog. Anyway, I've had to talk to her about that cat, because sometimes he leaves dead things on our front porch, mice or chipmunks or fuzzy bits that used to be alive, and that really upsets my wife. Can't have the wife upset, now can we? But I've never seen that teacher anywhere around here, and I think I would have. I consider myself the unofficial neighborhood watch, ha ha. If something was going on between those two, she kept it to herself. But teenagers are good at that. Keeping secrets."

—*Todd Rosentople, neighbor*

WOLF WOMAN

An hour later, we're in the car, our substitute father, Mr. Doctor, at the wheel. He's spoken exactly one sentence during the twenty-minute ride: "To Grandmother's house we go!"

We've been having dinner at Grandma's every Monday night since before I was born. We kept the tradition going even after my mom divorced my dad and we had to bring Mr. Doctor with us. Grandma Emmy and Grandpa Joe don't know what to make of Mr. Doctor; he's so dull in comparison to the rest of us. But Grandma and Grandpa don't seem to hold that against him.

When we get there, Grandma Emmy drags Mr. Doctor outside to show him the new fence they had installed in the backyard, basically because he's the only one boring enough to care about things like fences. Madge goes downstairs to play something slow and mournful on the piano in the basement. I hang in the kitchen with Grandpa Joe, who is stirring a big pot of sauce. We're all pretending that everything is 100 percent A-OK, that I'm a perfectly normal adolescent going through a perfectly normal adolescence.

"Well. I guess your sister's still obsessed with that funeral music," Grandpa says as the notes waft upstairs. "I wish she'd learn to play a cancan."

"She likes the funeral music. She says it cheers her up," I tell him. "So do all those war movies."

"Hmmm," says Grandpa Joe. He fought in a war and doesn't find anything about wars cheerful. "Does she still cry a lot?"

"All the time. When she's not breathing into lunch bags. She's got a new doctor, though. Mom is hoping this one will work. I'm not so sure. Madge hates him just like she hated the other ones."

Grandpa blinks. I'm not sure what they did with girls like Madge in his day. Gave them lobotomies, probably. Maybe that's something I'll suggest to Madge the next time she tries to kick my cat.

Grandpa hands me a spoon and waves at the pot of sauce on the stove. I stir it, smelling the garlic and oregano. He rips a hunk of bread off a loaf, dips it into the sauce, and hands it to me. I take a bite. It tastes a lot like ketchup with garlic and oregano, but I eat it so fast that the sauce gets all over my face. Such a lady.

"Good?"

"Good," I say.

He tries some. "Tastes like ketchup," he says.

"I like ketchup."

"Back in the day, we thought ketchup *was* tomato sauce. My mom put it on spaghetti. This was before the war. Before we knew any real Italians."

"We live in New Jersey. I can't imagine not knowing any Italians."

"Well, you also can't imagine not having a cell phone."

"True."

Grandma and Grandpa are old, but they're not *old* old. Not in spirit, anyway. They go out dancing every weekend. Grandma bowls and plays bingo, and Grandpa golfs and cooks. Well, he tries to cook. He took some lessons and experiments on his family. Grandma thinks this is funny and lets him. I help Grandpa sometimes, chopping vegetables, basting chickens, browning meatballs. Since I inherited my appetite from him, Grandpa Joe always lets me eat as much as I want without the weird judgmental faces. Good thing the food is getting better. Also that I am a connoisseur of crap.

"Paint anything new lately?" he asks.

I tell him about the substitute teacher, how she said my painting died on the canvas.

"She's just jealous that her paintings don't die on the canvas," he says.

"I don't think it was a compliment, Grandpa."

"Why not?" he says. "I thought art was supposed to be dramatic. Dying is pretty dramatic."

"I guess," I say, sighing. "But I did have a dream a while ago. It was pretty dramatic."

"Really? What kind of dream?"

"I was in this castle. All stone and stained glass and tap-estries. And there was a beautiful queen on the throne. She had long, silvery hair and a blue velvet dress. Little birds circled her head like a sort of crown, singing happy songs."

"Birds," he says.

"Yeah, birds. The only weird thing about the dream was her feet. She didn't have human feet. She had bird's feet. And they were orange."

"Interesting."

"It makes sense, though. The bird's feet, I mean. In the original 'Cinderella,' there wasn't any fairy godmother. It was a pair of magical birds that gave her the gown and the shoes and all that stuff. So I was thinking that I might paint her. If I can."

"What do you mean, if you can?"

"Sometimes what you have in your head doesn't come out on the canvas. Sometimes you don't even know where to start."

"But you're going to try?"

"Maybe."

"It certainly sounds out of the ordinary," he says. For Grandpa, anything out of the ordinary is a good thing. Works for me, because I'm not smart or driven like my sis-ter or mom; I'm not some straight-A machine. When I was little, Grandpa Joe was the one who went through my school folders piece by piece, examining every drawing, every construction paper report. Grandpa Joe is my biggest fan. He's always checking my web page for photos of any new paintings I've posted. He says it gives him something useful to do with the laptop my mom gave him for Christmas, which Grandma keeps unplugging because she's afraid it will set the house on fire.

He says, "I'll want to see that painting when it's finished."

"You're the only one. Well, you and . . ." I'm about to say Mr. Mymer, but I don't finish. I don't have to. Grandpa knows who I'm talking about. He's heard about Mr. Mymer a million times.

I think he might ask about Mr. Mymer, but he says, "Your mom wouldn't like your painting?"

"Are you kidding?" I say. "Things like that scare her. She can't understand why I don't paint normal pictures."

"What are normal pictures?"

"Sailing ships in tranquil harbors? Bunnies in bowties? Whiskers on kittens? Princesses with regular feet?"

"She's proud of you."

"She wants me to think about advertising as a possible career."

He laughs. "Your dad's an artist type and he did okay. Well, he did fine eventually. How is he?"

"Your guess is as good as mine."

"Why don't you call him up?"

"I have," I say. He would see us soon. Yes, he promised. Hannalore says hello. Hannalore can't wait to see us also. Which means Hannalore's in the process of interviewing huntsmen and has several promising candidates picked out. They will have to provide their own axes, and they will be required to bring her our bloody hearts after they murder us in the woods.

To my grandpa, I say: "Dad's busy."

"Shouldn't be too busy for you," he says.

I don't have to lie to Grandpa. "No, he shouldn't."

Grandpa always liked my father, even when Dad was barely making any money selling his miniatures at flea markets and Grandpa had to give him loans. Grandpa Joe said that too few people in the world know what they really want to do. He thought my dad was a lucky man simply because he knew what his passion was. Even something as odd as building little models.

But he's mad at Dad now, I can see that. He grabs the wooden spoon, tastes the sauce, and makes a face.

"Are you sure this is okay?"

"It's great."

"It's not too bitter? Doesn't need more sugar?"

"I like it the way it is."

"Hmmm," Grandpa Joe says. He coughs, pounding his chest.

● ● ●

The food is on the table, and we are at the table, when she walks in. No one would ever imagine that she and I were related. She's as big as I am small, with a pile of thick, dark hair, big hands, and man-sized feet. Bigger than Hannalore even, which might be why they hate each other.

Mom is pissed at me, but she tries to keep up appearances for Grandma and Grandpa. She kisses them both gently on the cheek, as if they're something that could be broken if loved too hard.

"Hey, Mom. Hey, Dad. Everything looks great." She tosses her coat and briefcase on the bench in the kitchen and takes a seat. We dig in. I heap my plate with spaghetti and meatballs, salad, and garlic bread. My mom, as tall as she is, takes one meatball and about three strands of spaghetti. My sister, after pigging out on Oreo crumbs and bread balls, eats only salad. As Madge picks through her lettuce, she talks about how, during wartime, people do plenty of normal stuff in addition to all the killing and the dying, and isn't that amazing? "People go to dances, listen to music, have babies, bicker over stupid things like where someone put the mug with the yellow happy face," she says. "This guy Noël Coward wrote a whole play after his apartment and office were destroyed by Nazi bombs, some comedy about a society guy whose marriage is haunted by the ghost of his first wife. It was a huge hit."

My mother is nodding uh-huh while frowning at Madge's greasy ponytail. You can see her wanting to ask about Madge's shower status. She is saved by Mr. Doctor, who tells a story of a fifth-grader who passed out while getting his braces adjusted for the first time. "We had to call the ambulance and everything," says Mr. Doctor. And everything.

I talk about Rumpelstiltskin. Not the "dies on the canvas moment," but the other ones. How she said Valerie Schenke's accidental spill looked like Jackson Pollock, how her heart ached when she looked into the breast-eyes of the pseudo-Picasso.

Grandma Emmy laughs. Madge nods. Mom says, "What kind of outfit is that supposed to be?"

I'm wearing my standard uniform: fishnets with a black skirt. My style is kind of punk-slash-goth-slash-early-Madonna—lots of netted items, filmy shirts and skirts, camisoles and corsets, a ton of layers. To change outfits, I usually replace the inner layer, say, the leggings under my skirt, and then move the other layers out, like sharks replace their teeth.

"What's wrong with my outfit?"

She stabs at her meatball as if it has offended her. "You look like a cross between a vampire and a saloon girl."

I twirl spaghetti around my fork. "You say that like it's bad."

"I don't like this . . ."

I fill the word in for her. "Attitude?"

She glares at me. Not like Madge, whose eyes and brain

and mouth are on fire. My mom's cold. Frozen. If you touch her, your skin will come off.

I say, "Anyway, I thought we were talking about my outfit."

"The outfit is part of the attitude."

I try to be funny. I try to keep up appearances, too. "Uh, Mom, we *do* have pictures of you when you were in high school. I seem to recall a troubled relationship with hair spray."

"I wonder if it's that . . . man."

My mother won't even speak his name. Mr. Mymer is now in the same league as Voldemort.

Grandma Emmy says, "Does anyone want any more spaghetti?"

Grandpa Joe says, "Maybe you should talk about this another time."

I say, "I've been wearing these kinds of clothes long before I met *Mr. Mymer.*"

"But since you've been in his class, you stay up all night painting those pictures."

"What's wrong with taking my art seriously?"

Mr. Doctor says, "I had another patient who brought his pet gerbil in his pocket. His name was Fred. The gerbil. Not the patient."

"I wish you'd pay this much attention to your other classes," my mother tells me. "You're in high school."

"So?"

"So I thought I told you to take that thing out of your nose."

"Non sequitur!" sings Madge.

"Dad said I could get my nose pierced."

"I don't care what he said. Besides, neither of you was invited to his million-dollar wedding. You could wear an Indian headdress and he wouldn't care."

I tap my nose ring, which isn't a ring but a tiny (fake) diamond. "Dad likes it. And he doesn't have any free time. He's working."

"Yeah, *now* he is." She tears into her lettuce. It is terrible, terrible lettuce. It is lettuce with an attitude. "I should have known he'd find success in building little toy houses."

I finish her thought. "Because he's such a child?"

"Finally, my little girl is learning," she says. "No stars in your eyes."

"Just in my nose."

She grabs the salad tongs from the table and waves them at me. "Which you will remove immediately or have removed for you."

And then dinner is done, the dishes swept from the table and washed by Grandma Emmy, who can't bear to sit still. Also, she wants to clear the table so that she and Mr. Doctor can play cards. She loves beating him at cards. Whenever he's too slow figuring out what he wants to do with his hand, she slaps her palm on the table and yells, "Come on!

I'm losing money!" It always makes Mr. Doctor jump. As they play, my mother looks through her work files, slashing with a red pen. My sister goes back to the piano and pounds out a dirge.

Grandpa suggests we get some air. It's cool outside but not cold. Smells clean. Grandpa takes the steps slowly, one at a time, gripping the rail. He says that at his age, one can never be too careful. "I don't want to fall on my bean and scramble the few brains I have left."

"You have plenty of brains left, and they're only slightly scrambled."

At the bottom of the stairs, he says, "And how are your brains these days?"

"Scrambled."

He says, more quietly now, "I'm asking you if you're all right."

I won't make a joke, not now, not to Grandpa Joe. "I'm not all right," I say, "but not because my teacher hurt me. Because people think he did. Mom thinks he did."

"She worries."

"She doesn't have to. Really. And neither do you."

I will him to believe me. I try to put my heart in my eyes. He watches me closely as I speak, then he nods. "Good enough."

When we're standing in the front yard, he takes some deep breaths of the cool October air. "Whew! Any more of that funeral music and I was going to have to make an appointment with the undertaker."

"Madge would be happy to go in your place."

"Don't say things like that," he says sharply.

"Sorry. I just meant . . . sorry."

Just as quickly, his tone softens. "That's some sky," he says. "Do you know why the sky is blue?"

"No. Do you?"

"Molecules in the air scatter blue light from the sun more than they scatter red or any other color in the spectrum. I saw that on a nature program."

"Uh-huh."

"Makes me dizzy, looking up like this. When you get to be my age, you'll know what I mean."

I look at his sparse gray hair, the bags under his eyes, the brown spots dotting his hands. I always forget how old he is. Eighty-something. More than sixty years older than me. Seems like forever. Grandpa came along before everything—before television, computers, cell phones, digital picture frames, iPods. I know a lot of old and not-so-old people who hate a lot of this stuff, who think the whole world was so much better before all the snotty little jerks came along and ruined it with their earbuds and their ringtones and their stupid, incomprehensible gadgets.

But not Grandpa. Grandpa blinks his papery eyelids, the eyes beneath them strong and green as olives. "Things change," he says.

I'm not sure if he's talking about Madge or Mr. Mymer or my dad or my mom or me, but it doesn't matter. "Promise?"

"Before you know it, Madge will stop playing that funeral music. She'll dance the tarantella and play the kazoo. You'll be off to college. You'll study Greek and Latin and art. You'll paint princesses with bird beaks. The world will be your oyster."

"I hate oysters."

"You'll travel. You'll go to France."

"Mom will never let me."

"By then, she won't have to let you. It will be your choice."

My choice? The idea is so remarkable that I can't even remark on it. I hold his still-strong hand as we admire the sky's skill with blue.

(*comments*)

"What do you want me to say? I can't believe she did anything wrong. She's a child. You want some answers, talk to that teacher. He's the adult, right? Tola's a good girl. A very good girl. Loves her grandma, the way it should be. What's that saying about the drummer? That one. She marches to the beat of her own drummer. What's bad about that? Nothing, I say. Nothing."

—*Emmeline King, maternal grandmother*

"I actually threw a dinner party in their honor. Never again. She and that appalling sister of hers insulted the décor. They insulted the food. They insulted their father. And they verbally brutalized me.

"So if you're asking whether I'm surprised at what happened, the answer is a definite no. I wouldn't put anything past either of those girls. And no wonder. Just look at their mother."

—*Hannalore Miller, stepmother*

"It was an adults-only occasion, so the girls weren't at the wedding. But that doesn't mean that they weren't supportive."

—*Richard Riley, father*

"Box turtles have more humanity than the woman my father was dumb enough to marry."

—*Tiffany Riley, sister*

GINGERBREAD

In bio, we are still gearing up for D-day. Dissection. We spend more time hearing about what we can't do with our pigs than what we can. Even though Mr. Anderson believes in personal freedom, even though he thinks it's our duty and our privilege to leave our mark on our landscape—in other words, destroy the ozone layer with hair spray and the water with lemon-fresh bleach if we darn well feel like it—he doesn't mean that it's our privilege to do whatever our little free hearts desire in his classroom.

"Democracy ends at the door, my friends. Touch someone else's pig, and you—and your lab partner—fail. *Molest* someone else's pig, and you and your lab partner fail. This is not a game."

Miles Rosentople says, "No molesting the pigs!" and tries to spear me with a pencil. Everyone laughs.

Mr. Anderson turns from the board to pin us with

his eyes. "What's so funny?"

I use Miles's pencil to sketch little piggies with their houses blown down.

In cooking, we have moved on from plain mayonnaise to flavored, a thrill for the entire class. We will be making blueberry mayonnaise, curry mayonnaise, wasabi mayonnaise. The Duck waddles around the large square tables, passing out copies of different mayonnaise recipes. Today, my partner and I get mango-chutney mayonnaise. My partner, Transformer Guy, grunts his approval. Or disgust. It's hard to tell. He only speaks in guttural noises and gestures.

I get out the measuring cups and bowls while Transformer Guy splits the recipe in half. The Duck gives a single egg to each team, setting it gently down on the table in front of us as if she had laid each one herself. The rest of the ingredients we have to fetch for ourselves. Salt, powdered mustard, sugar, cayenne pepper, lemon juice, olive oil, hot water, chutney, chives. Almost immediately, one of the teams drops their egg to the floor and the Duck squawks.

After we've gathered the ingredients, Transformer Guy and I read the rest of the recipe together: Beat yolks, salt, mustard, sugar, pepper, and lemon juice in a small bowl until very thick and pale yellow. Add about ¼ cup oil, drop by drop, as beating continues. Transformer Guy is happy. I think he's had much experience with beating.

I dump the stuff in a bowl, and he grabs a whisk and begins the vigorous mixing process. I drop in the oil. Drop, drop, drop.

D

R

O

P

"So," says Transformer Guy, "I read something about you."

What is this? Transformer Guy *speaks*? Super storms are gathering over North America. God will break California from the surface of the continent like someone breaking off a piece of chocolate. It will become its own floating paradise of underweight movie stars and dot-commers, like a fat-free Atlantis with superfast Wi-Fi. June's phone will apply for citizenship.

I find my voice. "Everyone's always hearing something about me."

"I didn't hear it, I read it." He begins beating again.

"Okay."

"Don't you want to know what it is?"

"Not particularly."

"I think you do."

"I really don't."

"I would."

"I'm not an industrial refrigerator from another planet."

"What?"

The Duck peers into our bowl. "The mixture should be thinner," she says. "Are you adding oil?"

"Yes," I say, holding up the greasy measuring cup.

The Duck scowls and moves on to the next team. Transformer Guy waits a minute, then says: "It's about Mr. Mymer. You know Mr. Mymer?"

"Yes, I know Mr. Mymer."

"Well?" he says.

"Well, what?"

"I heard you guys are . . ." he says, trailing off.

"Teacher and student?"

"No," he says.

"Mentor and protégé?"

"No," he says.

"Father and daughter? Mother and son? Singer and song?"

"No."

"Coffee and tea? Sugar and spice? Peanut butter and jelly?"

Transformer Guy just smiles knowingly.

I blurt: "Whatever it is, whatever you're thinking, it's not true, you idiot. Could you people be more stupid?"

Transformer Guy keeps smiling. He's a totally infuriating refrigerator. An appliance with an attitude. My mother would be appalled.

He says, "We know what you're like. You'll do anything. Probably 'cause you're short. You know. Overcompensating."

●●●

Overcompensating. That's the word Mr. Mymer used when I started showing up in his classroom at lunchtime way back when I was a freshman and the world was new. I didn't want to eat in the cafeteria, I said. It wasn't the food I hated; it was the people. Everyone was so *young* and so *dumb.* They never talked about anything interesting. The girls complained about how fat they were—no matter how skinny they were—and the guys made sex or fart jokes. I'd only been in school for four weeks, and already I wasn't sure how I was going to deal with four years if it.

"Fart jokes," I said, "are never funny."

Mr. Mymer laughed. "Oh, sometimes they're funny."

"When?"

"So there's not one person worth talking to in this whole school?"

"There's you."

"Thanks. But I meant a student, Tola."

"No. Well, there's my friend June. But she joined the chamber choir and has practice during lunch this semester."

"So you have to eat alone."

I'd had a fight with my other friend, Chelsea Patrick. She tried to convince me to go to the mall to meet some guy she'd been talking to online, a guy named Spit. She said he would give us weed or pills or whatever we wanted. She thought this was good news.

I wasn't about to go meet some creep named Spit to get mystery drugs. Chelsea called me a wuss and went by herself.

So I'd tried to eat alone. I'd tried to ignore the swirling chatter of "I feel so fat today!" and "Would you tap that? I'd tap that." I tried to do what Mr. Mymer had said to do: draw what we know in order to learn what we didn't know. In my sketchbook, I drew a group of kids sitting at a table, bugs flying from their mouths. I drew until one of them shouted, "What are you *staring* at, Tola? Why are you always *staring* at everyone?"

To Mr. Mymer, I said, "I like to be alone."

"But not all the time."

I glanced behind me. There were a few students working quietly at easels or at the potter's wheels, lost in the whale songs of their iPods. "I heard that you let people come in and work during lunchtime," I said. "I thought maybe I could eat here. And then I can get some work done."

"That's fine with me," he said. "But is that the real reason you want to be here? To work?"

"What other reason is there?"

"I don't know. Maybe you don't hate people as much as you say. Maybe you're overcompensating because you're shy. Sometimes it's hard to come to high school and—"

I cut him off. "I am *not* shy."

"There's nothing wrong with it. Plenty of people are shy."

"And plenty of people don't like fart jokes."

"I just think it's a good idea to try to make some friends in the real world. You kids rely too much on the internet for a social life."

"Now you sound old."

"I *am* old."

"Mr. Mymer, you're nice and everything, but don't ever become a psychologist. You don't have the skills."

He nodded, giving me a lopsided sort of grin. "Okay, Tola. Whatever you say." His T-shirt had a message, CANCEL MY SUBSCRIPTION. I DON'T NEED YOUR ISSUES. I dumped my backpack on the nearest table and pulled out my lunch.

We have a new sub in art class. She, unlike Rumpelstiltskin, the former sub, loves the colors I used in *Rapunzel Gets a Cat* but has no use for the subject. As a matter of fact, she has no use for any subjects. She shows us photographs of canvases painted entirely blue. And some painted entirely red. A few that look like checkerboards. She says they are "brilliant explorations of pure color." She says they are "bold and confrontational, humorous and witty." She gives us paint and challenges us to do the same. I leave my canvas blank and stare out the window. When she questions me, I tell her the piece is called *Irony*. She doesn't find this humorous and witty as much as confrontational. She sends me to the principal's office.

The principal isn't happy to see me.

Later, in the cafeteria, I find out why Transformer Guy broke his silence; June shows me on her NASA phone.

TheTruthAboutTolaRiley.blogspot.com. The posts are snippets of different local newspaper articles; random, pointless videos from *Oprah* and *Dr. Phil*; the opinions of random people who say they know me. In other words, the moronic howls of the attention-starved and insane. According to most of them, I'm the one who's crazy. They think I should be expelled for sleeping around. Or they think I should be expelled for lying about sleeping around. They say the art room was some sort of sex room, that students hooked up in the supply closet. They think Mr. Mymer should be fired. Or maybe promoted. They want to know if someone will be making a movie and who will star as me. They agree that I shouldn't be allowed to make any money from the movie. It wouldn't be fair. They don't know who should get to keep the money. Maybe Mr. Mymer. Maybe the school. Maybe it should be split among the students, because they've had to suffer, too. The students are suffering!

"We are surrounded by lunatics," I say. As I say this, Seven passes by the table. He frowns, as if he thinks I'm talking about him. I've always had impeccable timing.

June and I are eating lunch again. Which means I am the only one eating. June doesn't look up from her screen. "You already knew that."

I am distracted by Seven's eyes, which are a silvery green. "Knew what?"

"Knew that we are surrounded by lunatics."

"What are you doing?" I say.

"Adding a comment to this stupid blog."

"What kind of comment?"

"The kind that says you didn't do anything wrong and they should all get lives."

"Oh," I say. I realize that I'm surprised that June believes me. Or at least wants to leave a comment that says she does. "Maybe we could hang out this weekend," I say.

She shakes her head. "Can't. Mom signed me up for a retreat."

"What kind of retreat?"

Her faces squinches up. "Young Leaders of Tomorrow. And if you make fun of me, I'm going to kill you."

"I guess it will look good on college applications," I say.

"I guess," she says. "I'd rather be out with my dad." June's dad is a locksmith; he has a set of lock picks and everything. When she's not texting or attending seminars, she works with her dad, picking locks, replacing them when someone's house has been robbed or when they're afraid that their ex-husband is going in and out of the house. She says working with her dad makes her feel like a TV detective.

"So, what are you going to do?"

"This weekend?"

"About this." She points to the screen.

"I can't stop them from putting up a website."

"Didn't your lawyer make you take down your blog?"

"Yeah," I say.

"So why do these cheese monkeys get to have a blog and you don't?"

"I don't know," I say.

"You should at least find out whose blog it is."

"Yeah, okay," I say. What I really want is to prick my finger on a spindle and sleep for a hundred years. I want to wake up in a whole different storybook.

A crumpled piece of paper hits me in the chest. I scoop it from the floor and read it.

ART TEACHERS DO IT IN FULL COLOR!

I hand it to June. "This is for you."

She reads the note and scowls at Pete Santorini, Ben Grossman, and Alex Nobody-Can-Pronounce-His-Last-Name three tables away. "Creative," she says, "but not funny at the moment." The three of them look down at their shoes and shuffle their feet, the perfect picture of shame. Except for the snickering.

Something—a hand—drops like a spider on my shoulder. June's face tells me who it belongs to. I give my shoulder a little shake. Her hand doesn't move. I shake my shoulder again. She gives me a light squeeze.

I turn as much as I can. Not much, because she's strong, and she's putting all her weight on me. "Let me go, Chelsea," I say. I can't see her because she's behind me, but I can picture her: black hair chopped in a mullet, Ramones shirt, ripped tights, boots made for kicking.

And I can smell her. Deodorant and sweat and hot dogs.

"How are you doing, Tola?"

"Get off."

"This whole thing must be really hard." She actually sounds sympathetic. I want to throw up.

"I said get off." I try to sound strong, but I sound like the wuss she said I was. Chelsea's minions—Tweedledum and Tweedledumber, also wearing their fake punkwear—laugh.

She squeezes even tighter, tight enough to dig her fingernails in. "You poor thing. I feel so sorry for you."

"Come on, Chelsea," June says.

"Come on, Chelsea," Chelsea mimics. "Shut up and text. I'm sure your mommy would want to know who you're having lunch with."

June blinks furiously behind her retro glasses but shuts up. Chelsea Patrick can do that to anyone. Once, during a snowstorm, she called the school superintendent at five A.M. and told him he should cancel classes. He yelled at Chelsea, saying she was an "obnoxious little witch in need of supervision" and a bunch of other things. Chelsea taped the conversation and put it—and the superintendent's private phone number—on the internet. Kids cranked the superintendent day and night. The newspapers went crazy. Chelsea's mother complained at the treatment of her daughter. The superintendent was forced to apologize to Chelsea and her mom. Last year, he moved to another district.

"I've heard teachers talking about you and Mymer," Chelsea says. "Nobody believes a word you say."

"Because of what you told them."

"Who? Me?"

"You were at the museum. I heard you laughing. I know it was you."

"You. Are. So. Silly." Chelsea punctuates each word with a sharp slap on my back. "Why would I say anything about you? Why would I even care?" She giggles as if she's never heard anything so strange. "Then again," she says, "you never know what you can get people to believe." And then she turns and marches away, the minions scrambling to keep up.

(*comments*)

"You don't know anything about anything. All you losers spreading this crap about Tola Riley need to get a life! Put down the cell, join a club, read a book, watch a movie, make out with your boyfriend/girlfriend, pet your dog, and *stop* being such a bunch of pathetic, useless A-holes!"

—*June Leon, classmate*

"The teachers don't know what to do when she gets defiant. She was sent to my office again today. To be honest, I don't think it's appropriate to be alone with her. I've been keeping the door open so that my secretary is a witness. Not that she's done anything . . . provocative, you see, but to protect us both. I think that I will recommend she see the school psychologist from now on. She's a woman. The psychologist, I mean."

—*Thomas Zwieback, principal*

"I started messing with people online a few years ago. MySpace, blogs, whatever. All you had to do was find the person who was the touchiest, the whiniest, the most defensive about everything. The person who used all the capital letters and the !!!!! Who took it all personally. And you'd mess with them. Dis their favorite books or movies. Pretend you were a hot guy and tell them how much you wanted them, then turn around and call them an ugly slut. Hilarious. The drama! The heartbreak! And they'd never even met the guy. LOL.

"There was this one girl on MySpace, a real loser. The kind of girl who posted all this bad love poetry and pictures of herself in bikini tops. I made a page for an emo guy I called Razor and then friended her. 'Razor' told her how hot she was and how much 'he' loved her poetry. She fell for the whole thing. Thought she had a new boyfriend. Wrote all these pathetic emails about what she'd do for him when she met him. Right up until 'Razor' posted that he was dumping her for a cheerleader at school and that her poetry sucked.

"As far as Tola Riley goes, I haven't even gotten started."

—*Chelsea Patrick, classmate*

SKIN

At home, Madge is collapsed like a tent on the couch, watching *Saving Private Ryan*. When I try to talk to her, she waves her hand in irritation. "Go away," she says. "This is the good part." I look at the screen. A soldier is ever so slowly stabbing another soldier in the heart. As one kills and one dies, they each murmur in a language the other doesn't understand. They are close enough to kiss.

I go outside and call for Pib. It's a cold day, colder than normal for this time of year, and I have to shove my hands in the pockets of my jeans to keep them warm. The brown leaves from Pib's favorite tree crackle under my feet. The trees shake their naked arms at me. Sometimes Pib doesn't show right away; sometimes he has other things to do. I shout his name and stamp my feet to keep the blood flowing. My father would have joked that Pib, named after Puss in Boots, was off fetching rabbits on behalf of his real master, the Marquis de Carabas. I would have said that Pib was always his own master. He's definitely his own master today, because he won't come even after I've spent ten minutes shouting his name.

I give up and go inside for snacks. I eat a grilled cheese, four cookies, and a couple of pickles. Then I take a stack of crackers and slather each one with a thick layer of butter. I arrange the crackers on a plate—presentation is important—and am about to bring it to my room when the doorbell rings. I freeze where I stand. The calls from reporters are down to a trickle since my mom changed the numbers. And only a few have been dumb or assholic enough to come to the door. I leave the crackers in the kitchen and yell down the stairs.

"Madge! Get the door!"

"No!" she says.

"But I'm not allowed to answer it!"

"So don't!"

"But shouldn't we find out who it is?"

"Who cares?"

I tiptoe to the door, which is stupid, because whoever it is probably heard the shrieking. I put my eye to the peephole, but all I can see is a white blur. A plaintive meow pierces my ears. I yank open the door.

"Pib?" I say.

Pib's climbed the iron lattice on the outside of the screen door and is splayed eye-level. He yowls again.

A voice behind him says, "I think he's stuck."

Carefully, I open the screen door just enough to slip out-side. Seven Chillman stands there, fattened by a puffy blue coat. "I didn't want to touch him," he says. "I was afraid I'd hurt him if I tried to pull him off."

I don't answer. I pluck Pib from the lattice. He meows but lets me hold him. He's soaking wet.

"Where did you find him?" I say.

"In my yard. I live a few blocks up the hill that way." He points in the direction of the backyard. "Your cat was fish-ing for koi."

"For what?"

"Big goldfish. We have a pond."

It was then that I noticed Seven was soaking wet, too, his coat drip-drip-dripping on the concrete.

"You're all wet."

"Yeah. Well. Your cat really didn't want to be caught."

Pib growls in agreement.

"How did you know where I live?"

"I'm psychic."

"What?"

"He's wearing a tag," Seven says. "Where'd you get the name Pib from?"

"Puss in Boots," I say.

"I remember that story. There's a princess."

"There's always a princess."

"And a prince."

"There's always a prince. There are more princes than princesses."

"I don't think so."

Out of the corner of my eye, I see Mr. Rosentople raking leaves in his front yard, close to our driveway. I'm glad it's getting dark. You don't want to spend precious minutes trying not to stare at the thick fringe of curls that spring out of the collar of his sweater.

Also, who rakes leaves in the dark?

"Hi, Tola!" Mr. Rosentople says cheerfully. "Keeping an eye on that cat, I see."

"Just like I said."

"My wife thanks you. My flower beds thank you." Mr. Rosentople eyes Seven curiously. Seven salutes.

"How's your mom?" Mr. Rosentople says.

"Fine," I say.

"Tell her I said hello."

"We've got to get inside now, Mr. Rosentople. My friend is freezing."

"Oh, okay."

I pull Seven inside the house and slam the door shut.

"I guess we don't like that guy," Seven says.

I don't answer. Pib leaps from my arms to the floor. He shakes each of his paws delicately, like a woman drying her nail polish.

"That's funny," Seven says. "That's what my mom does when she's trying to dry her nail polish."

I stare at him. I feel a completely crazy urge to touch him. His hair. His cheek. His hand. Of course, I've felt this way before. Nothing good ever comes of it.

"What's going on?" Madge says, padding into the hallway. "Why is there a wet guy in our house?"

"Hello," says Seven.

Madge squints. "I know you. You're Chilly's little brother,
aren't you? From Willow Park High School?"

"Yeah," he says.

"Your brother's kind of an ass."

He laughs. "Sometimes."

"Are you an ass?"

"Sometimes, I guess. But I try not to be."

She nods. "I suppose that's something. You should give
Tola your clothes."

We both gape at her.

"To put in the dryer, pervs. Get him some of Dad's old
stuff to wear. It's in the back of Mom's closet."

"Right," I say.

"Pervs," she says.

"That's okay," Seven says. "I can wash my clothes at
home."

"At least give her the coat. She can dry that. We don't
need you getting pneumonia and suing us. We have enough
problems as it is, in case you haven't heard."

"I've heard. There was a reporter parked across the street.
He asked me if I knew you."

"What did you say?"

"I said, *Ego operor non narro English.*"

"What language is that?"

"Latin. My mom made me take it."

"Useful," says Madge.

Seven shrugs out of the coat. "She said it would help me with my SATs."

"Did it?"

"No. I failed Latin. And I'm not taking the SATs." He hands the coat to me. Turns out it's only half wet. One arm of the coat and part of the front.

"I had to lie down at the edge of the pond to reach in," he explains to Madge. "The cat went after one of my fish. Then the fish went after the cat."

"It's a fish-eat-cat world, that's what I always say," chirps Madge. To me, she says, "Mom gets home soon. If she catches your friend here, you'll both be at the bottom of the pond." She turns back to Seven. "Nice meeting you." She snatches the coat from my hands. A few seconds later, I hear the whir of the dryer.

"Well," Seven says. "She's . . ."

"Psychotic?"

"I was going to say *interesting*."

"You have an interesting definition of interesting."

"I do, actually."

From the other room, Madge bellows, "Pervs!"

"Are you thirsty? I could get you something to drink."

"Okay," he says.

Seven follows me to the kitchen. Pib follows Seven.

Before I do anything else, I grab a dish towel and dry Pib off. He retreats under the table to groom in private.

"What do you want? Coke? Water? Milk?"

"Do you have any coffee?"

"Uh . . ."

"I see a coffeepot on the counter."

Great. I don't know how to make coffee.

"It's okay. I know how to make it," he says.

It's my mom's coffeepot. She doesn't like anyone using it. "Sure," I say. I get the coffee from the cabinet and slide it over to him.

"Do you have filters?"

"Yeah. I think." I dig around in the cabinets until I find a filter, and I hand it over. I watch as he fills the pot with water and then measures out the grounds. Soon, the kitchen smells like the color brown. I don't like coffee, but I love the color brown. It is warm and chocolaty and . . .

"So," he says.

"So."

"It smells like brown in here, doesn't it?"

I can barely speak. "Yes."

He points to his own face, at his brown skin. "Makes sense."

"I guess it does," I say.

"But then again, you're brown, too, in the blood, any-way."

"I am?"

"If you go back far enough, everyone is African."

"They are?"

"Yes. The skeletons of the first humans were discovered in Africa. We're all descendants."

"I didn't know that."

"I saw it on one of those nature programs."

I laugh. "You sound like my grandpa."

"He's African American?"

"Well, yeah, if you go back far enough," I say, smiling. "But I meant to say that he likes 'nature programs.'"

The coffeepot stops percolating. I pour the coffee into a mug and put it on the table with milk and sugar. As I set the mug in front of him, I smell something underneath the coffee. Something thick and sweet.

"Why do you smell like vanilla?"

"I like to rub Twinkies under my arms."

"Isn't that sticky?"

"A little. I'm going to try fudge next."

"That could work."

"Are you going to tell me about Mr. Mymer?"

My stomach squeezes in on itself. "Are you asking for that reporter out there? Did he pay you? Are you trying to be famous or something? Start your own blog?"

"No."

"So then why are you asking?"

"I want to know."

"Why?"

"Because."

"Because why?"

He wraps his hands around the mug. "I want to put you in my pocket."

"What?"

"You heard me."

"I don't know what you mean."

"You know what I mean."

Pib slinks out from under the table and winds himself around Seven's legs. I feel dizzy. My heart has little wings on it, and they're flap-flap-flapping away.

He clears his throat. "Do you want to go to a movie or something?"

The wings stop flapping. "I can't. I'm sort of under house arrest."

"Till when?"

"Till pigs fly and hell freezes over."

"Soon, then."

"Any minute."

He drinks about a quarter of the coffee, and then fills the mug to the brim with milk. One spoonful of sugar. "I don't believe any of the stuff they're saying about you. I never did."

"Never? How long is never?"

"A long time."

I want to say, *So why are you here now? Why not yesterday, why not months or years ago, when you could have really done some good, when you could have stopped me?*

But Pib takes the opportunity to flop onto his back and show Seven his belly, which Seven dutifully scratches. "Ferocious," says Seven. He closes one eye and peers up at me with the other. In the dim light, his eye looks as silvery and otherworldly as Pib's. I wonder if I should paint him with a cat's diamond-shaped pupil.

"I won't mind if you painted me. I think it would be cool."

"I . . ." I trail off, suddenly sapped of the energy to speak. How does he see inside my head? How did he know I want to paint him? But it's true. The tips of my fingers twitch. They want brushes. They want paint. They want the scratch of bristle on canvas.

The cat's blinking, first at me and then at Seven, probably wondering why people just don't go into heat and get it over with.

"Tola?"

It's my mom. In my trance, I must have missed the sound of the garage door.

"I heard voices. Is someone here?" Her voice has the shrill edge it gets when something is happening that she does not want to be happening.

I sigh. "Yeah, Mom. A friend."

She appears at the top of the steps, still wearing her coat and carrying her briefcase. "Hello. I'm Tola's mom." She does not sound friendly. She is not rolling out the welcome mat.

"Seven Chillman," he says. He stands and holds out his hand.

She can do nothing but shake. "Seven? As in the number Seven?"

"Right."

"That's . . . intriguing. Does it stand for something?"

"Yes," says Seven, who then smiles politely. My mom frowns.

"Pib fell in a pond and Seven found him," I say. "He brought him back here for us."

"You're kidding," my mom says. "A pond?"

"In my yard. We have koi."

"That cat is crazy." Mom looks at the coffeepot, at the mug on the table.

Seven holds up the mug. "Tola made me coffee. There's some left, if you want it. Unless coffee keeps you up at night."

My mom makes several strangled noises, all of which indicate she's trying to figure out what to say to this.

"My mom's always tired when she comes home from work," Seven says. "Sometimes I make her coffee. I used to, anyway. She can't drink it anymore. She says she won't sleep."

I recognize this tactic from cop movies and thrillers. People who talk about their families can sometimes convince the bad guys not to kill them.

Mom unwinds her scarf, takes off her coat. She's torn. Yes, I am in Protective Custody, I am the Girl Locked in the Tower, but then here's a guy who's my age, and clean, and polite, and maybe I'll end up being normal after all, and I'll stop having clandestine affairs with people old enough to be my dad. What's a mom to do?

She knows what to do: "I appreciate you bringing back our cat, Seven, but now is not the best time for Tola to have company. I'm sure you understand."

"Yes. Right," says Seven. "I should get going, anyway. Do you want the mug in the sink or the dishwasher?"

My mom looks at him strangely. "The sink is fine."

I get his coat out of the dryer and walk him to the door.

"I'd really like to go to the movies or the art gallery or wherever you arty types go when, you know, hell freezes over," he says, pulling on the coat.

"That could be a while."

"I can wait."

He calls up the stairs: "Nice meeting you, Ms. Riley!"

There's a pause because my mother doesn't like to be caught eavesdropping. Her voice wafts down the stairs. "You, too."

I open the door. He turns. As if we really are a prince and princess in a fairy tale, he takes my hand and brings it to his lips. The kiss is warm and soft and longer than it needs to be. He keeps his spectacular eyes on me the whole time he does it. My breath catches in my throat and is trapped there, a solid thing. It's almost as if he can sense it, that moist knot of breath, because I can feel his smile on my fingers.

● ● ●

After he's gone, my mother appears at the top of the stairs again. She's been working on her entrances and exits. They get more and more seamless, more and more dreamlike. Poof! Instant mom.

"He seemed like a nice young man," she says, with an emphasis on the word *young*.

My hand tingles where Seven's lips touched it; I don't want to talk. I want to lie in my bed and replay that kiss in my head over and over and over again until I stop time.

She must know this. As she's always telling us, she was once a teenager, too, even if we can't imagine it. "I'm making that chicken you like for dinner," she says, a truce. "The one with the apricot sauce and rice."

"Okay," I say. "Broccoli, too?"

"Of course."

"Good."

This is more code, more nontalking talking. The rules: She won't mention that she believes I've had an affair with a teacher. She won't mention she's trying to ruin his life forever. I won't mention that I hate her for it.

Later, during dinner, a fight breaks out between Madge and Mom over Madge's therapist, a fight in which Madge wants to know why *I'm* not seeing a therapist, too, if Mom's so convinced I'm a victim of abuse. Madge wants to know if Mom still intends to "out" me at the school-board meeting, and how that would be abuse on top of abuse. Mom says that everyone knows who I am. And that it's more important that she, Mom, fights for her daughter and everyone else's daughters. Anyway, Mom says, the fight isn't "about Tola." My sister says that every fight is "about Tola." Mr. Doctor asks if there's any more apricot sauce for the chicken. Tola, who's sick of being the subject of so many ongoing/online conversations that seem to have no relationship to what's actually happened to her, to what's actually happening, retires to her room with her crazy cat.

Besides Seven, only three guys have kissed me, and a fourth did something that resembled kissing but shouldn't even count. The first guy, Raul, I met in day camp when I was twelve. I was almost normal then, way before I pierced my nose and dyed my hair and generally made everyone crazy. Every morning for a week, I stole two cigarettes from my mom, who was trying to quit at the time, and shared them with Raul at the end of the day, after most of the other kids had been picked up. His tongue was weird and gluey, and he tasted like burned toast, so I told him that the cigarettes had made me sick and I had to go to the bathroom to throw up, which I did, twice.

The second was a guy I met on the boardwalk one night when we were on vacation at the Jersey shore; he never told me his name. I went for a walk on the beach with him, and he picked me up and carried me around as if we were being filmed for a deodorant commercial and then ended up making out on the beach. He reached under my shirt and tried to get into my bra, but I stopped him; now, I'm not sure why. It's not like I had anything in there, anyway. We made out some more and then went home. The next day, I went to talk to him at the boardwalk game where he worked, the one where you put the little rubber frogs on a stand and pound a lever with a hammer and try to get the frogs to land on lily pads. He looked up and, with not one iota of recognition in his voice, said, "Three frogs for a dollar."

The third guy, Billy, was this senior in my high school. I saw him playing football in the street with a couple of his friends and made sure that I intercepted one of the passes. What I mean is that I walked into the middle of the game because I was lost in a daydream and got hit in the head with the ball. We went out for two months, which was an eternity considering that the only reason we were attracted to each other was because he thought it was cool to go out with someone freaky, and I thought it was cool to go out with someone semipopular. It wasn't long before he started complaining about my hair and my clothes, and I didn't want to go to parties filled with the young and the witless. We got bored talking to each other on the phone, and he started telling me these involved, incredibly detailed stories about his favorite pastime, hunting. I mean, who hunts in New Jersey? I broke up with him after he gave me a forty-five-minute lecture on the proper way to gut a deer.

Which was partially the reason I made out with a girl. June and I were sitting alone in Mr. Mymer's art room eating lunch freshman year, lamenting the fact that since I'd broken up with Billy, neither of us had boyfriends. And since we didn't see any reasonable prospects around, we were destined to be alone and lonely for the rest of our lives, and wasn't that completely pathetic? Then June suggested that maybe there was another alternative: girls. We listed the advantages. Girls are generally cleaner, safer, smaller, and can't get you pregnant. Most of them don't do stupid things like play Guitar Hero for fourteen hours straight or attach a chain to one of those huge blue mailboxes and try to pull it behind his dad's car the way Miles Rosentople did, which got him arrested.

On paper, dating girls seemed to be a fantastic idea, much better and more practical than dating guys. June asked me if I'd ever kissed a girl before, which neither of us had, not for real. So, since there was no one around, and since we figured no one would care anyway, we tried it. Unfortunately, we picked the exact moment when the vice principal came looking for Mr. Mymer to discuss the reason he hadn't turned in his grades yet. And, unfortunately, the vice principal *did* seem to care, a lot, and wasn't at all reassured by June's assertions that human sexuality is on a continuum, and that almost everyone, maybe even the vice principal himself, was bi, if they were only evolved enough to admit it.

Anyway, the last guy was John MacGuire, the one who shouldn't even count. A couple of months ago, he invited me over for a party. He was cute enough and played the drums in the school orchestra, so I thought he'd be okay. When I got to his house, I found out there wasn't any party, or, rather, *I* was the party. I'm not sure what he was thinking. Maybe he'd heard about me and June and thought he was living life in the middle of a porno, or maybe he thought that since I was a social misfit, I must be desperate. He practically jumped me as soon as I sat down on the couch. The kiss didn't even qualify as a kiss; it felt more like someone grinding a big raw steak into my face. After one and a half seconds, he was simultaneously jamming his hands up my shirt and tugging at my jeans. I clocked him with what I thought was a vase but turned out to be a fishbowl. Water spilled everywhere, and a single goldfish flip-flopped on the couch cushion. While John whined that I could have just said no and that he'd sue me if I'd given him a concussion, I found a Dixie cup, filled it with water, and plunked the fish in. Then I took him home and gave him to Madge. She named him John MacGuire. One day we came home from school to find that Pib had eaten him, leaving only the tail lying like a tiny fan on Madge's dresser. We had a funeral ceremony, dropping the tail into the toilet bowl. "Poor John MacGuire," said Madge as the tail swirled around the bowl. "Another innocent sacrificed for someone else's sin."

The moon watches over me the way she always does. I pop a fresh canvas on the easel under the skylight. I stare at the surface, white as a sunspot. Pib lolls on my bed, blinking rhythmically. Like he's trying to tell me something in code.

The canvas is clean and white. I look over my paints and start grabbing tubes, spitting little blobs onto my palette, mashing them with the brush. Raw umber, burnt umber, raw sienna, a tiny hint of red oxide. To that I add titanium and a wash of iridescent gold.

Yes. There it is. Glimmering. Liquid. Alive.

I fill a whole canvas with the color of his skin.

(*comments*)

"I lied. I didn't find Pib in the koi pond. I found him on my doorstep. He had a chipmunk in his mouth, but the chipmunk wasn't dead. It didn't even look hurt. Pib wouldn't let go of it, so I sprayed him with the garden hose. Not a lot, not hard, but just enough to make him let go of the chipmunk and get myself soaked. The chipmunk was so dazed, he ran over to me and sat on my shoe for a minute, not a drop of blood on him. Then he ran under the bushes. Pib didn't care about the chipmunk. He trotted down the driveway. I thought he was leaving, but he kept stopping to look behind him, as if he wanted me to follow. So I followed. I thought it might be weird to tell Tola that I stalked her cat to her house, but that's what I did. I almost don't believe it myself."

—*Seven Chillman, classmate*

"Mom wants me to stop watching my favorite movies, as if that will make everything better. What's wrong with *The Pianist? Saving Private Ryan? Das Boot?* I'm supposed to be watching romantic comedies that are neither romantic nor comic? I'm supposed to be watching *Twilight?* Let me tell you something, the pretty, sparkly vampires aren't coming to save us. We're not worthy. We're not special. We don't even smell good."

—*Tiffany Riley, sister*

"My ex-wife called to tell me about the boy. I told her that it would be good for Tola to have a boyfriend her own age. That maybe the boy could help Tola move on from this whole thing. My ex accused me of trying to sweep everything under the rug. To pretend that everything's okay when it's not. She was furious when I said I couldn't come to the schoolboard meeting. I have a new job. I can't take the time off.

"Believe me, I know things are not okay."

—*Richard Riley, father*

"Someone's got to do something about that bloody animal."

—*Todd Rosentople, neighbor*

"Meow."

—*Pib, the cat*

BAD APPLE

The school-board meeting is held in a nondescript square building, the interior of which is painted a lovely shade of snot. We wander around until we find the right room, a small, dark auditorium that would seem more appropriate for hangings than for school-board meetings. In the front of the room is a long table with a series of microphones and some sweating pitchers of water on it.

Even the pitchers are nervous.

The whole place is packed with people who look like the parents on police dramas—pinched, confused, waiting for someone to tell them that it was all just a nightmare and they can go back to sleep now. They turn and look at me as we walk into the room.

There she is.

That's the girl.

She looks so young.

The poor thing.

Is she wearing a costume?

Maybe she's in a play.

They're all so young.

What's wrong with her hair?

We look for seats, but since the room is packed, we find ourselves squeezed into the back row. Mr. Mymer is nowhere to be seen. Chelsea Patrick is nowhere to be seen. The school board arrives one at a time, settling themselves in front of microphones, shifting papers around. After a while, the board president bangs his gavel for the meeting to commence. But they don't want to tackle the hot topic up front. They want to ease themselves into it.

First, the school-board members discuss the school bus route and whether it should be expanded a quarter-mile to the west. Then there's the matter of the after-school program, which leads to discussion of the costs of extra staff and supplies. An alarm system for the school. And then some talk about the budget in general, which won't have to be approved for months. I yearn to stare out the window and appear stupid, but there are no windows. When I start to nod off, my mother elbows me.

Finally, the board president, a man whose huge head and stiff plastic hair make him look like a life-size doll, opens up the floor to the audience.

The crowd begins to buzz as a woman makes her way to the podium set up in front of the board. She does not mention me or Mr. Mymer. Apparently, there are other evils in the universe besides crazy kids and abusive teachers.

There are . . .

. . . books.

"My name is Serena Patrick, and I'm a parent and a taxpayer," she says. She looks familiar. Serena Patrick. Patrick? Chelsea Patrick's mom? She was always so nice, serving lemonade and cookies every time I came over.

But Father Time has pulled his tricks. She's got those puffy cheeks and crazy trout lips that scream, "I HAVE HAD THE FAT OF CADAVERS INJECTED INTO MY FACE!" Plus, the Botox appears to have gone to her brain.

"I'd like to read you a list of profanities that appear in this book," she says. "Twenty uses of the words *bastard* or *bitch*, forty-nine uses of the S-word, and thirty-four uses of the F-word. And that's just one book in the stack I pulled from the library shelves. The *school* library shelves. We don't allow children to use this sort of language in the school hallways, so why are we allowing them to read books laced with obscenities?"

A man in a rumpled suit whispers, "What the goddamn kind of crap is this? Shee-it."

Someone else hisses, "That's not funny, you know. The world is going to . . ."

"Hell?"

Ms. Patrick taps the stack of books she brought to the podium with her. "Some of these also contain drinking, drugs, violence, sex—the book I talked about earlier mentions oral sex eleven times! I don't know about the other parents in this room, but I think it's hard enough dealing with the likes of MTV without having the school participate in the degradation of our culture."

I have to wonder if she's met her own daughter. Chelsea Patrick is walking proof of the degradation of our culture.

Snarky guy in the rumpled suit, louder now: "These are high-school kids, not kindergartners."

The president bangs his gavel: "Please, sir. If you'd like to speak, you'll have to take a turn at the podium."

Ms. Patrick aims a hot glare over her shoulder. "A quarter of the children attending the school are only fourteen or fifteen years old." She turns to face the board again. "Fourteen-year-olds simply don't have the critical-thinking skills to digest this sort of material. They want to try out everything they read." Her voice quavers and I realize that she's absolutely terrified. All the parents look like that. And I think: Why are they so scared of us? What do they think we're going to do? What did *they* do when they were our age?

Mom's mouth is tied off in a smirk, but she must be terrified, too. Otherwise, why would she do this to me?

"If you'll let me interrupt for a second," says the president. "Did you find all the books in your daughter's backpack, or did you simply start pulling books off the shelves and reading them at random?"

"Well, no. I found a website. Concerned Parents for Control of Our Libraries. CPCOL." CPCOL: It's a pharmaceutical company! It's a decongestant! It's an antibiotic for Botox-induced brain infections!

The board president rubs his face so hard it's as if he's trying to scrub his whiskers off. "Oh. Well. We appreciate your comments and we're going to take them all seriously."

"Very seriously," adds another board member, a woman wearing a shade of yellow normally found only on tropical fish. "Can I see that book about the oral sex?"

The president frowns at her.

"What?" says Tropical Yellow. "I'm concerned, too."

The president shakes his head and turns back to Ms. Patrick. "What we need you to do is give us a list of the books you're having trouble with, and we will reevaluate their inclusion in the school library."

A sharp voice knifes the air. "Oh, for the love of Jesus!"

The crowd turns. Ms. Esme, our high-school librarian, is standing in the middle of the aisle with her hands on her hips. She stares at each of the board members in turn, then at Chelsea Patrick's mom. She turns and strides from the room, the *clip* of her heels on the floor telling us exactly what she thinks of us.

"There's a novel in the school library about a student having an affair with a teacher!" Ms. Patrick shouts after her, holding up yet another book with an apple on the cover. Bad apples everywhere. "Now we have a problem with a student and a teacher." Her eyes drift around the room until she finds me and my mom. "There's *surely* a parenting problem there," she says, "but, still, how do you defend this? How? I really want to know. I do. . . ." Ms. Patrick trails off, absently patting the stacks in front of her. "I really, really do."

That's enough excitement for one school-board meeting, right? No. There's more to come.

Next up, Mom.

Yay.

"My name is Anita Riley Baldini, and I'm the parent of a student at Willow Park High School. Recently, my daughter, who is a junior, was involved in a questionable relationship with her art teacher.

"All due respect to Ms. Patrick, but I can't blame books for my family's situation. And I don't blame my daughter, who is young and confused and can't be held entirely accountable. I *do* blame myself—for not noticing the problem soon enough. I *do* blame the teacher in question, who shouldn't be allowed near students under the age of eighteen. I *do* blame the school board for keeping this man on staff. And I *do* blame the teachers' union for defending him.

"Many of you are probably wondering why I broke my silence here. Why I brought my daughter with me. What I hope to prove by going public. Well, my daughter's and my family's privacy has already been compromised by scandal-hungry newspapers and amoral teenagers blogging online.

We have been exposed to the most vicious sort of gossip and innuendo. I can't safeguard my child's privacy as much as I'd like to. But what I can do is tell people to pay attention to the signs of trouble in your own children. My daughter got more and more secretive. She paid less and less attention to her other classes. She got more defiant at home. I told myself that this was normal, that teenagers dress in ridiculous outfits, dye their hair funny colors, and defy their parents. I told myself to be patient; I thought this was the way of things. I was fooling myself. Let's not fool *ourselves*.

"I'm incensed that this teacher, Mr. Mymer, is living off of my tax money after he took advantage of my daughter, a vulnerable young girl. I demand that this teacher, Al Mymer, who has been on suspension with pay, be fired immediately before he hurts anyone else. Thank you."

When my mom sits down, she doesn't even look at me. She's as rigid and virtuous as a nun.

Three other parents get up and denounce my art teacher. One of them says that his T-shirts are suggestive, especially the one that said SQUIRRELS CAN'T BE TRUSTED. (What is *squirrel* a euphemism for? Only the teenagers know for sure.) A single guy stands up to defend Mr. Mymer, but the board quickly realizes that he's gotten Mr. Mymer mixed up with Mr. Mason, the shop teacher.

"Oh," the guy says. "Well. Maybe you can give him a

raise or something. He helped my son make a really great bookcase. We use it for all our videos."

"What are you doing?" my mother hisses when I stand. The audience buzzes. Blood beats in my ears; my stomach feels like someone poured concrete down my throat. I wish I were six hundred feet tall. I wish I'd saved the "pixie" haircut till senior year. I wish I could fill the room with my presence, make people forget how small I am.

I bend the microphone as far as it will go and clear my throat. "My name is Tola Riley, and I'm a junior at Willow Park High School," I say.

"Could you speak into the mic, please?" says one of the board members. "We can't quite hear you."

The mic is already as low as it can go, so I stand on tiptoe to get closer to it. "My name is Tola Riley," I say, louder. "I'm the girl who is supposedly having an affair with Mr. Mymer." I take a second to let that sink in. "But I'm not having an affair with Mr. Mymer. We never met in his office or his car or his apartment the way people are saying we did. We haven't been dating for years. We just happened to go to the same museum on the same day, the way you bump into someone at the mall. I don't know what your 'witness' says she saw, but she's lying. We weren't holding hands or whatever. We never exchanged any presents. He wasn't doing anything but teaching me about art, and I wasn't doing anything but learning. This isn't Mr. Mymer's fault. He's a great guy and a great teacher. He never did anything to hurt me. And I don't know why everyone keeps saying he did."

I stop talking and wait for the response.

There is nothing.

No group exhalation. No sigh of relief. No oh-my-god-we-were-wrongs. It's so quiet that I can hear the low hum of the microphone and the hush of my own breath.

The school-board president: "I'm sure that took a lot of courage, Tola. We'll certainly take your comments under consideration."

"Wait," I say. "What do you mean, you'll take my comments under consideration?"

"We're going to give this a lot of thought. And we're going to sort through your and others' statements, the police reports, et cetera. All of it's important."

"But I'm supposedly the abused party. And I'm telling you that I wasn't abused. Shouldn't my comments count more than everyone else's?"

The board members glance at one another, at the papers in front of them. They shift and squirm. Some take sips of water.

The board president: "Thank you very much for speaking with us today."

I find my chair and sit down.

Mr. Mymer isn't at the meeting, but his union rep is. The union rep says:

1. The teacher denies that there was an affair.
2. The student denies that there was an affair.
3. The school administration and the police didn't find one shred of proof of an affair.
4. Ergo, there was no affair.
5. Ergo ergo, this is nothing but a witch hunt designed to besmirch the reputation of a committed, talented teacher with fifteen years of experience.
6. Triple ergo, the board has no choice but to reinstate Mr. Mymer and issue a formal apology.
7. Period.
8. End of story.
9. Finis.

By this time, the crowd is ready for the finis. But the school board has other ideas. They vote to consider the comments from the community and the most recent information and announce their decision at the next school-board meeting, or maybe the one after that, or maybe during the next ice age. They wish us a happy Thanksgiving and tell us all to drive safely if we're traveling.

When the meeting is over, the people file slowly out of the building. Ms. Patrick glares at my mom as if it's her fault that I went so wrong. But the other women give my mom smiles of encouragement; they grip her arm or pat her shoulder.

They are mothers, and they understand.

(*comments*)

"My daughter says that the girl is not the innocent little thing her mother seems to believe she is. She's been hanging around that teacher for two years before anyone noticed what was going on. Thank goodness that my daughter was brave enough to call school officials after she saw them at that museum, not that I'm advertising it. No one in this town would thank her. Especially that girl's mother. You'd think that she's the only mother in the world with a child who's been hurt. There are a lot of children who've been hurt. There are strip-poker parties and rainbow parties. Kids making their own porn with cell phones. Cyber-bullying. What will it take for parents to see what's going on right under their noses?"

—*Serena Patrick, parent of classmate*

"I met a guy named Spit online. He was the real deal. Totally hot. Totally cool. I wanted to meet him so bad. But I was still young then, and chicken. I asked

Tola to come with me. She said she couldn't. Some friend. I went by myself anyway.

"When I met him IRL, it was like BAM! Fireworks. Maybe because he's older, I don't know. We used to wait for my mom to go to sleep, and then he'd crawl in my window. We'd mess around online most of the night. Spit could get email addresses, snail-mail addresses, and credit card numbers. We signed people up for porn sites. We ordered books on bomb making and weight loss and erectile dysfunction and sent them to people's houses. We found the website of this born-again Christian dude, so we had a blow-up doll delivered to his church in his name.

"People called us trolls. But that's okay. It just means we were stronger than everyone else."

—Chelsea Patrick, classmate

BALONEY

It's Grandpa Joe's first time cooking a turkey, so he gets one of those giant birds so monstrous with hormones that, if it were alive, it wouldn't be able to stand up by itself. It comes complete with a magic button that tells you when the turkey is done. We worship at the altar of the oven, waiting for the button to pop. It never does. Finally, we get the brilliant idea to find the meat thermometer. By the time we take the turkey out, it's so overcooked, it's lost about three pounds and its puny wings have fallen off.

"Good thing I made a lot of gravy," Grandpa Joe says.

We sit down at the table. For our Thanksgiving dinner, we are serving the desiccated monster turkey, stuffing, mashed potatoes, sweet potatoes, green-bean casserole, cranberries from a can, biscuits from a can, and barely suppressed rage.

We are still doing the nontalking talking, but it's more *non* than it is *talking*. Mom hasn't been able to look at me since the school-board meeting, but for today she manages to blather on about her job as a marketing manager, how she's only one person, how her bosses think they can get blood from a stone, and how unfair it is that people in Europe get six weeks of vacation when she has to content herself with three. Mr. Doctor tells a story of a kid who threw up on him while they were trying to get molds of the kid's teeth for braces. (Mr. Doctor seems to think this is the kind of funny story one relates while others are eating sweet potatoes.) Madge spits out the latest injustice at the community college, where she is taking a course on the Holocaust. The injustice has something to do with getting yelled at for being late to class. She gets mad when I tell her the way not to get yelled at for being late is to not be late.

"This is college," she says. "It's not supposed to matter if I'm late or not."

"Who told you that?" my mom says.

"Besides," says Madge, "I had a good reason."

"What reason?" says Mom, but Madge won't say, clams up tight. And then Mom gets mad because Madge won't say and reminds her that her very expensive therapist, an M.D. *and* a Ph.D., suggested that Madge share more with her family, that if we understood what was going on in her head, we might relate to her better. Madge pokes at her turkey. Mr. Doctor suddenly finds the cranberry dressing utterly fascinating and reads the ingredients from the can under his breath. Grandma Emmy starts to clear the plates even though none of us is finished, and slaps my hand when I grab a slab of turkey with my fingers. Grandpa Joe starts to cough, pounding his chest.

"I don't like the sound of that cough, Dad," my mom says.

"I don't like it, either," Grandpa Joe says between coughs. "But it's nothing a little cough syrup won't cure. What can you do?"

"You can go to the doctor."

Grandpa Joe rolls his eyes.

"Don't roll your eyes at me, Dad." Mom sounds as if she's talking to Madge or me instead of her own father, and everyone stops poking or clearing or muttering to stare at her. "You should have that looked at. Where's your doctor's number? I'm calling him right now."

"It's Thanksgiving, Anita," Grandpa Joe says. "And it's just a cough. There's no need to overreact."

"I am *not* overreacting," my mom barks. "I'm simply doing what has to be done. I don't know why people don't understand that. There are things that need to be done, and no one else seems to be interested in doing them. So I'm doing them, and I don't care who hates me for it. Now, what's that number, Dad?"

After a joyous holiday weekend that I spent mostly hiding in my room, I'm back at school. The board meeting

hasn't improved my social standing. But it has electrified
TheTruthAboutTolaRiley.blogspot.com. June shows me
on the NASA phone. There are hundreds of new comments.
There's a reporter who wants to write a book about student-
teacher love affairs. She plans to include a chapter on me.
Commenters debate a title for the book. I debate moving to
Mexico. My stomach churns, trying to eat itself.

Due to the rotating schedule, art is my first class. I bring
in the brown canvas I call *The Skin of the Marquis de Carabas*.
The new sub, an older man who appears to have colored
his hair with black shoe polish, takes one look and sniffs,
"I prefer more art in my art." He sets up a pear and a large
wheel of cheese on his desk. We spend the rest of the period
sketching them. In my drawing, the pear is cut up in slices,
a knife plunged into the center of the cheese.

Later, I have math. Everyone else in the eleventh grade
has some sort of precalculus. I have a class called Math-
ematics and You. It should be called Nothing Will Ever
Add Up for You, Loser. Mrs. Worksheet is trying to get us
to understand the real meaning of big numbers. She asks us
how long it would take for us to reach 1 million pennies
if we got one penny a second. Answer? Eleven and a half
hours. Then she had us calculate how long it would take to
reach 1 billion pennies. Thirty-two years. We also discover
that 1 billion pennies will fit into five school buses and that

we haven't even lived for a billion seconds yet. It just feels that way.

When the bell rings, I run to biology. Time to dissect the poor baby pigs. The pigs were delivered to our classroom in large tanks of formaldehyde. Me and my lab partner, LaDonna Rowan, name our pig Baloney in honor of Mr. Anderson.

Because our school system has a fondness for alphabetical seating, I've been paired with LaDonna Rowan in class since the sixth grade, and she has spent all these years perfecting her life plan:

1. Graduate from high school ranked number five or better.
2. Attend Cornell University as her father and her father's father and her father's sister-in-law's brother had.
3. Get into a first-rate or any other medical school.
4. Become a world-class heart or plastic surgeon (whichever makes the most money).

I have no idea how LaDonna is going to achieve her grand plan if she's stuck in Science for Dummies like me. But I look down at that poor fetal pig staked on the wax dissecting tray, sickly pink and lumpy as a pickle. "Considering you're going to be the surgeon, LaDonna," I say, "you might as well make the first incision. You should probably make all the incisions."

So, as LaDonna Rowan hunches over Baloney, breathing in the toxic fumes and poking around in the little pig belly, trying to live up to her own legend, I sit there on my lab stool, holding my nose. I feel woozy. It's not the fumes or the sight of all those tiny pig innards. It's that meeting. It's my mom. It's *me*, dragging myself from class to class the same way I always have. How is it possible that I stood up in front of everyone and said, "No, no, no, I am not hurt, I am not a victim," and they refuse to hear? How can all those people at TheTruthAboutTolaRiley keep telling stories using my name, if they're not really about me? Am I so small, so insignificant that my own story doesn't need me anymore?

I break down and ask for the bathroom pass. I probably look ill, so Mr. Anderson doesn't argue. I slip into the nearest girls' room. It stinks of cigarettes, but it's empty. I splash my face with water and dry it with a scratchy paper towel. I decide that my green hair is ridiculous. That's why no one would listen to me. Who would listen to a girl with green hair?

And Seven. Well. He must have felt sorry for me. A green-haired girl with a crazy cat and a crazier family. He'd be wise to stay far, far away.

I would.

I crumple the paper towel and toss it in the can. No sense hiding in the bathroom. No sense hiding anywhere.

I throw open the bathroom door.

And bounce off the huge chest of Chelsea Patrick. She fumbles with her cell phone and almost drops it.

"What the hell are you doing?" she hisses. Then she sees it's me. And smiles. "Look who it is! The little fairy whore."

My blood starts to hum. "Get out of my way."

She tips her head and considers me. "No."

I move to go around her, but she just steps in front of me. I try again, and again she blocks me.

"Stop," I say.

"Stop what?"

"We used to be friends. Why are you doing this?"

"Doing what?" she says.

I want to scream, *Screwing with my head! Screwing with my life!* But I just stand there, my fists clenched so hard that my fingernails cut into my skin.

"You should be sorry," she says.

"Sorry for what?"

She holds out her cell. "Speak into the microphone."

I don't care. "Sorry for what? I didn't do anything."

She smiles. "You've done lots of things. I have proof of some of them."

"Proof?" What kind of proof? What is she talking about?

"Or maybe I don't," she says.

I feel like a punctured tire. "Look, I'm sorry if I hurt your feelings. People grow apart," I say. "It's just what happens."

"That's nice," she says. "You hear that on a talk show?"

"I'm going to tell the school board that it was you. That you made the whole thing up about me and Mr. Mymer."

"I did? Are you sure?" she says, her grin even wider. "Aw,

don't look so sad." She slips the cell phone in her pocket.

Before I know what she's going to do, she reaches around and grabs me by the back of the neck. She yanks me close. I try to push away, but she's too strong. With her free hand, she pops the cap off a red lipstick. "Stop wiggling," she says. "You're going to ruin it." She holds me still as she scrawls something across my cheeks and mouth and rams two dots into my forehead.

She holds me still as she inspects her handiwork. "Much better," she says. She lets go. I'm too shocked to move. She pulls her cell from her back pocket and takes a picture of me. Then she strolls off, daring me to try to do something while her back is turned.

I don't. I run into the bathroom.

She's made me into a smiley face.

Have a nice day.

When I get back to class, Mr. Anderson snatches the pass from my hand. He stares at my face—flushed and damp from the scrubbing. "If you're going to be sick again, take yourself to the nurse. If not, join your lab partner and try to make yourself useful."

I try to control my breathing as I watch Miles Rosentople take his fetal pig and pull its legs over its head.

"Yogi Kudu!" he says. He named his pig after a yogi that had been featured on YouTube (the yogi folded himself into a suitcase). Miles Rosentople thinks he's very, very funny.

"Try to get the arms over the head, too. He's not a real yogi until he can do that," I say. Miles Rosentople does what I tell him, just like he'd eaten worms when he was eight and tried to light his own farts on fire when he was eleven and stole painkillers from his dad when he was thirteen—all on dares. I know about Miles Rosentople because his dad would come over to our house and complain to my mom about it. Sometimes sans shirt. In addition to the hairiest back you've ever seen, he also sports droopy little old-guy boobs.

Shudder. I don't want to think about Mr. Rosentople's old-guy boobs. I don't want to think at all. I feel for the victims in this sad excuse for a biology class. Looks like the *CSI* version of "The Three Little Pigs." The pig that LaDonna is hacking at stares at me with its dead eyes. *Help me*, the eyes say.

Then they say, *Oh, never mind. I'm already dead.*

"Are you okay, Tola?" LaDonna wants to know.

"Fine," I say.

The pig keeps talking. *When I grew up, I wanted to be in a petting zoo. But no one wants to pet the pigs. Too dirty. But we're smart, you know. As smart as a three-year-old. Smarter. I myself am a genius. I was just thinking, for example, that if everyone's so convinced you're such a delinquent, why not start acting like one? Show them! A performance piece to beat them all.*

Miles is having a hard time twisting the pig's arms behind its head because they're so short, and his lab partner, Tim Corcoran, is getting annoyed.

"We're gonna fail if you keep doing that," Tim says.

"Nah," says Miles. "You only fail if you molest other people's pigs. Mr. Anderson didn't say anything about molesting
your own pig."

LaDonna looks up. "You're the pig," she says.

"Oink, oink," he says. "Kiss my curly tail." He waggles
the twisted pig at LaDonna, who scowls and goes back to
Baloney. For a future surgeon, her hands aren't too steady.
Baloney looks like he's been attacked by a pack of angry kindergartners armed with grapefruit spoons.

"Okay, my friends, time to wrap it up!" says Mr. Anderson.
"All pigs in their pens."

LaDonna pulls the pins out of Baloney's legs, closes the
flaps on his belly, and ties the plastic tag that identified him
around one of his feet. Then she brings the tray up and slips
him back into one of the tanks. Miles is still struggling with
Yogi Kudu.

"Don't worry about it," he says to Tim, who's wrapped
up everything wrappable and watches anxiously as Miles
pulls the pins from the pig. "I'm not going to do anything
to the pig."

"You already broke both its arms," says Tim.

"We had to break the arms to pin them to the tray anyway. Forget it."

Just then the bell rings, and Mr. Anderson yells impatiently, "Rosentople! Corcoran! Let's go!"

"Go on, Tim, I'll finish it," Miles says.

"I'll stay and help him," I say. Tim's even more anxious but backs away from us as if we've just pulled knives on him.

"Okay," he says. "But don't . . . don't twist him up anymore."

"Oh, man, just get out of here already!" Miles says. Tim turns and walks out the door, followed closely by LaDonna, who glances back at me with one eyebrow cocked, like *What are you up to?*

"Bye, guys!" I say, waving. "See you!"

Miles closes Yogi's belly flaps. "What are you hanging around here for?"

Mr. Anderson is busy shuffling papers at the front of the room, and kids are streaming in for the next period, talking and laughing. I suddenly feel like I'm standing on a cliff overlooking a deep, dark ocean and my mind is whispering: *Come on, you know you want to. Just a few more inches and you'll walk right off the edge.*

"I think we should kidnap one of the pigs," I say, feeling like some other person, some evil fairy bent on revenge. Even my tongue has a strange tart taste it didn't have before.

Miles doesn't say anything; he just drops his pig into one of the tanks and comes back to the lab table to get his books.

"Come on," I say. "It will be funny! We'll leave a ransom note."

"I don't know. We'll fail if we're caught."

"You're not chicken, are you?"

"Chicken. Yeah," he says. "I'm so chicken." He cocks his eyebrow at me the same way LaDonna did before she left the classroom. "You want to kidnap one of the pigs."

"Yeah."

"*You,*" he says again.

"Is it so hard to believe?"

"I remember when you were the hall monitor in first grade."

"I remember when you were caught in the playground trying to light your farts on fire," I say, trying very hard not to visualize that as I say it. "I remember you burned your butt so badly, you had to go to the hospital."

This annoys him. "Which pig?"

"I don't know. Jason's?"

"Nah." Miles shakes his head. "He's too stoned to notice."

"Bridget Fisher's?"

"That could be funny, but . . . we need someone even more uptight."

"Okay. Why don't we just kidnap Baloney, then? LaDonna will have a fit."

"You want to kidnap your own pig."

"Yeah! Now that would be funny," I say.

"You mean it will wreck LaDonna's grade-point average."

"Not if we don't get caught. And who would ever suspect me of kidnapping my own pig?"

"When?"

"How about today, after school?"

"Okay. You better be here," he says. He grabs his books. "I didn't know you were like this."

"Like what?"

"I didn't believe what people said about you."

"That's funny. I believe everything they said about you."

He snorts. "See you after school."

It's Mr. Anderson who catches us, just as we're dropping a sealed plastic bag with a ransom note into the tank where Baloney had been.

(comments)

"My friend Angela said her friend Priscilla said that her boyfriend saw Tola with Mr. Mymer in the art room and he was all over her. You know what I mean. And she wasn't complaining.

"I've been her lab partner since middle school, and she's always been nuts. Never pays attention to the teachers. Always scribbling weird little drawings in her notebook. Makes me do all the work. Not that I *can't* do the work. I plan on being a doctor. But still. It's sort of unfair to be paired with someone so unambitious for so long. She could be ruining my future career.

"I think the administration should be looking into that."

—LaDonna Rowan, *classmate*

"I'm not going to apologize. I'm not going to sit here and say, 'Oh no, I hurt someone's poor little feelings and I'm so so sorry.' One time, Spit left me alone with a couple of his friends. He fell asleep in the other room. He told me later that they just wanted to find out what my natural hair color was.

"I got over it. Shit happens to everybody. Sometimes it happens to you."

—Chelsea Patrick, classmate

ANYWHERE
AND EVERYWHERE

"Where did you hide the pig, Tola?"

This is the question they keep asking me, as if the answer will give them all the answers they ever needed.

"There was a ransom note," I say. "Twenty bucks and I'll tell you."

"There are sanitation issues here."

Before we dropped the ransom note into the tank, I'd taken the hall pass again and hid the pig in the trophy case in the front of the school. I think about suggesting that they hire June's dad to put in better locks. Instead, I say: "Ask Miles."

This frustrates them. They've probably already asked Miles, and he hasn't talked, either. Which strikes me as incredibly funny.

I'm the only one who's amused. Me, the principal, Mr. Anderson, the school psychologist, and my mom are all stuffed in a tiny conference room off the principal's office.

Nobody seems to be having a good time.

"Tell them where the pig is, Tola," Mom says. Normally, she sits perfectly straight in chairs. Today, she slumps as if she can't get the energy up to cross her ankles. She mutters, "I cannot believe what my life has turned into. This isn't a life. This is a TV show. Saying things like 'Tell them where the pig is.' What kind of dialogue is that? I need a new writer."

The school psychologist frowns at my mom, and my mom stares back, daring her to say something psychological.

The principal says, "Tola will fail biology."

Mom says, "That is unacceptable."

Mr. Anderson: "I laid out the rules. Mess with the pigs, and you and your lab partner fail. I couldn't have been clearer. Your daughter chose to violate those rules. There are consequences."

"I don't think the consequences have to be so severe, considering the circumstances," my mother says. "This will go on her permanent record."

"Are those records really permanent?" I say. "I mean, like, you post a photo of yourself topless and drunk on Facebook and that image floats around cyberspace forever, and suddenly you're forty years old and lose your job because your boss is using it as his screensaver. But are these permanent records the same? Really? I was just curious."

"I'm sorry I ever played those Baby Einstein videos when you were little," my mom says. "I'm sorry you learned how to speak."

I can't help it: I laugh. The psychologist is horrified. I have a feeling she'll be putting in a call to Child Protective Services. I'm not sure they can remove children from their parents because of excessive sarcasm, though.

"There," says Mr. Anderson. "She doesn't appear to be feeling any remorse. So I think the punishment is perfectly reasonable. And her lab partner will also fail. Lab partners live and die as a team."

Now the psychologist is horrified yet again. She doesn't know who in the room is the most horrifying. "*Live* and *die*?" she says.

I feel bad about LaDonna. Truth is, I wasn't even thinking about her. I'm not sure I was *thinking* at all. I decide that this must be my problem. The not thinking.

I say, "LaDonna had nothing to do with this."

"Doesn't matter," says Mr. Anderson. "She goes down, too."

The school psychologist: "Goes *down*?"

"And it was my idea, not Miles's. He shouldn't get in trouble, either." When I say it, I say it to my mom to gauge her reaction. She doesn't blink.

"I think we can make some exceptions this time," says the principal. Mr. Anderson opens his mouth, but the principal puts his hand up. "LaDonna won't be penalized."

"Thank you," I say. I don't need LaDonna hating me. I don't need to get anyone else in trouble for anything I've done.

"We'll figure out later what Miles's punishment will be.

But Tola will be given an F for this semester and will not be allowed back in Mr. Anderson's class. She will be in a study instead and will have to make up biology over the summer."

I have another idea. "I'll tell you where the pig is if you give Mr. Mymer his job back."

"Tola!" my mom says.

"One doesn't have anything to do with the other," says Mr. Anderson. His lips are curled away from his teeth as if I disgust him.

"Well, your class doesn't have much to do with life or death, but you seem to think it does."

Mr. Anderson turns bright red, but before he can start demanding that I be court-martialed, my mom says, "My daughter is experiencing significant emotional distress—"

The psychologist cuts her off. "Obviously! Probably due to the fact that—"

"*If you'll let me finish,*" says my mother, in that tone that means if the woman doesn't shut the hell up, Mom will have everyone buried up to their heads in the desert and let loose the fire ants. "Tola is experiencing significant emotional distress due to the fact she was taken advantage of by a predator."

"Mom, will you *please* stop! We're not on *Dateline*."

"We're very sorry, Mrs. Riley. Very sorry. I can't tell you how sorry—"

"Well, sorry doesn't fix the situation, does it? She's lost her father—"

"I haven't lost my father," I say.

"He's not here, is he?" she snaps. "This is an extremely difficult time for my whole family. I'm doing my best to keep it together and I believe the situation will improve, but I would appreciate a little more sympathy and cooperation from you people. I do know that teenagers are old enough to suffer the consequences of their mistakes, but I also know that she is a *minor* and that she was *abused* by one of *your staff*!"

The principal is silent for a few seconds. "What do you suggest?"

"I don't want an F to appear on her report card. She'll take the summer class to make up the work, but no Fs. And I don't want her record to include any suspensions, either, if that's what you're thinking."

The principal considers this. "I think that can be arranged. But she'll have to see the school psychologist."

Mr. Anderson barks, "Kids today can't just do whatever—"

"Mr. Anderson, you can get back to your students now," the principal says.

"But—"

"Now," says the principal.

Mr. Anderson storms out. I think he's contemplating rejoining the marines. The slamming door echoes in the little conference room.

"Thank you," says my mom. "And for my part, I can reassure you that Tola won't be acting out again. Will you, Tola?"

But she's not asking, and I'm not promising anything.

• • •

I'm excused for the day. The ride home with Mom is quiet, but the kind of quiet that's filled with all the things you really want to say but can't. I wonder if that's something I can paint. Every once in a while my mom swipes at her eyes and sniffs. When I ask if she's okay, she laughs and says, "Peachy."

Later that night, she asks me, "What are you trying to do to me, Tola? What are you trying to do?"

Madge has a new hobby. In addition to watching war movies, reading the latest research on psychiatric medication, screaming at Pib, and ignoring my mom's pleas for better communication, she's now a faithful reader of TheTruthAboutTolaRiley blog. (Mom had it shut down, but it popped up again and again in different forms and on different sites.) Madge reads the news articles quoting me and Mom at the school-board meeting. She reads about how Mr. Mymer and I were "observed" by another student "acting in an intimate manner," which makes me picture a middle-aged couple crammed in a grimy bathroom, cleaning out each other's ears with Q-tips.

The comments describe something you'd see on late-night TV or YouTube, complete with bad behavior in broom closets and lots of inappropriate language. In one of them, Mr. Mymer isn't a Mr., he's a Mrs., and we're hot lesbians in luv. In another, I'm a twelve-year-old immigrant boy from the

Philippines and Mr. Mymer is a twice-married, fifty-three-year-old father of seven. I stole a fetal pig, the post said, because it reminded me of the baby pigs I ate back home.

"Things were bad enough for you," Madge says, "and then you go and mess with Mr. Anderson. What is up with that? You're such an idiot."

Rather than making an artistic statement, or even a rebellious one, the pignapping has confirmed everyone's worst opinions of me. Do-anything, say-anything Tola Riley. I'm not allowed to be online anymore, so I can only imagine what's happening in other places on the Web, how the collective has examined and reexamined the evidence, the articles and the blogs and the texts that have been passed around; how they have all decided together what must have happened to me. I think about how nice that must be, to feel so sure of your own judgments, basically because no one is allowed to have different ones.

"But then most people at school are idiots, too. Nobody can decide anything for themselves anymore," Madge is saying. "It's all about groupthink."

I can't even remember where this started, when I became this outcast. Did it begin when people discovered I could eat more than a football player? When I outran Josh Beck? When I told Chelsea Patrick that I wouldn't go to the mall to meet some dealer named Spit?

"I dumped my Facebook," Madge says. "I couldn't stand it anymore."

"Couldn't stand what?"

"Do you ever listen when someone is talking to you? You're so annoying. It's like you're trapped in your own head all the time. The world doesn't revolve around you, you know. There *are* other people in the world," she says. She mercilessly pounds on the computer keys. "Wait a minute. There's something new here. You have a blog."

"Isn't that what you've been reading?"

"No, I mean *you* have your own blog. Someone claiming to be you."

"What are you talking about?"

"Listen to this: *To all you haters out there, this is Tola Riley. The* real *Tola Riley. I just want to set the record straight once and for all. Al Mymer didn't hurt me. He didn't molest me. He never touched me, okay? He's not that stupid. He knew everyone would freak out if he did.*

"*I'll be honest. I wanted him to. Man, did I want him to! Anywhere and everywhere and over and over and over.*

"*But this is not some stupid high-school fling. He loves me. So we're waiting till I turn eighteen. Then we're free to do whatever we want, and no one can stop us. Not my mom, not this stupid school, no one.*"

"I didn't write that," I say, my face sizzling. "I did *not* write that." But I did write things like it. Once, a long time ago, when Chelsea dared me to, I pretended to be a guy and wrote a couple of messages to some sad girl on MySpace. I didn't think it would hurt anyone, not really. But it did. It must have.

"They can trace all the computer stuff, so if you didn't write it, they'll know. We can tell Mom and she'll have the lawyer threaten them."

"A lot of good that will do," I say. "It will just pop up again somewhere else."

She bites her lip. "Unless you ditched school and used a computer at the public library or something."

"I didn't! Why would I do that?"

"I don't know. I'm just saying that if you did—"

"I thought you believed me."

"I *do* believe you."

"Then why are you saying this stuff?"

"I'm telling you what's on this blog, idiot. Why are you getting all mad at me?" She slams the computer shut. "You should be mad at Mom. You should hate her guts. Look what she did to you! She accused you of hooking up with a teacher in front of the whole world! After what *she* did!" She throws up her hands.

Now I'm completely confused. "Wait, what did she do?"

"Never mind."

"You can't say something like that and then say 'never mind.'"

"Yes, I can."

"No," I say, taking the computer away, "you can't."

"Fine. Mom made out with Mr. Rosentople."

"She *what*?"

"It's why he keeps coming over here, babbling about the

cat. He still wants to see Mom."

"But . . . how?" I say. "When?"

"A while ago. Right before Dad left. I had my window open," Madge continues, "and I heard your stupid cat yelling. So I went to find out what he was yelling about. I went outside. The meows seem to be coming from Mr. Rosentople's yard. I wasn't about to climb the fence, so I just cut around it by using the woods out back. From the trees, I saw them. Kissing.

"At first, I didn't get it. Then I almost threw up right there. I ran back home. Pib was waiting for me by the outdoor grill, yowling like someone had slammed his tail in a door. Stupid cat."

I sit perfectly still, thinking. "Maybe it wasn't what it looked like."

"It was," Madge says. "I saw it."

"Well, maybe he was the one who kissed her."

"Who cares who kissed who?"

"I think it's important," I say. "I think it's *very* important."

"No, it isn't."

"Why didn't you tell me this when it happened?"

"You were young."

"I was fourteen, not four."

"Yeah, well." She grabs a pen from my desk and writes the words PUNCH DRUNK on her jeans. She draws a little fist. And another. And another. "Mom didn't think it was a good idea to tell you, either. She asked me not to."

"She *knows* you saw?"

"Yeah. Do you think I'd let that one go?"

"What did she say about it?"

Madge crinkles her brows. "Some stupid excuse about it not being what I thought, blah blah blah."

"You don't believe her?"

"Look, what's *very* important is that Dad left right after that, okay? Mom is not the ethical queen she says she is." She pauses. "Why are you defending her? What's wrong with you?"

I say, "Did you ever talk about it with your therapist?"

"Are you kidding?" she says. "He'd just give me an assignment."

"An assignment? What are you talking about?"

"That's the kind of therapist he is. I get these little jobs or tasks that are supposed to help me. Like, say, if I were having a problem shopping in the grocery store, like if I were agoraphobic or something, he might give me the task of walking in the entrance and then walking out again. Then, the week after, he'd have me walk up and down one aisle. Then, two. Like that."

"Do you have problems shopping in grocery stores?"

"No, it's just an example! You are being so weird! Every reaction you have is all wrong! And everyone thinks I'm the crazy one."

"Not everyone."

"Please," she spits. "You don't even try to understand what I'm going through."

I'm about to ask what *Madge* is going through, with her straight As and her gap year and the fact that no one is writing talk-show-inspired blogs about *her*, but for once I stop myself. I see the red eyes, the dark circles draped underneath. She's going through something. Just because I don't understand it doesn't mean it's not real. She has a paper bag hanging out of her back pocket. She's exhausted. For the first time, I wonder how much she's sleeping. If she's sleeping at all.

"What kind of task would he give you about Mr. Rosentople?"

"Run him over with the car."

"You'd have to drive for that," I say.

"I'd get Mr. Doctor to run him over."

"Does it count if you use a proxy?"

"Proxy? Have you been studying your vocab?"

"Mr. Lambright rubbed off some, I guess."

"Mr. Lambright. I liked Mr. Lambright. I miss him."

Her tone sounds wistful, like she really means this. "You miss Mr. Lambright?"

"I miss writing five-paragraph essays. I miss topic sentences and supporting statements. I miss integrating relevant quotes with appropriate notations. And I miss conclusions. You don't know how much I miss conclusions." She sits up and starts to wheeze. I pull the paper bag from her pocket. She hunches over it, elbows on knees, the bag crackling.

• • •

(comments)

"Tola's mother and I have been neighbors and friends
for a very long time. She is a beautiful woman. But
nothing improper ever occurred. I don't know where
you heard that. Where did you hear that?"

—*Todd Rosentople, neighbor*

"My dad's totally into the lady next door. Tola's
mom. Has been for years. The whole block knows it.
I always thought that Tola knew it, too. He makes an
ass of himself all the time, lurking in the yard, spying
over the fence. What a screwup. Even the reporters
covering that Mymer thing look at him funny.

"My mom denies it all. But then, she likes her
wine.

"I hate them both."

—*Miles Rosentople, classmate*

"My daughter called and asked if she could spend
Thanksgiving with me. I had to tell her that I was

traveling to Germany to visit my wife's family for a few weeks. My daughter was very upset, as you can imagine.

"Back when I got engaged for the second time, my daughter told me that she thought it was great and that she just wanted me to be happy. But that's not true, is it? Kids don't care if you're unhappy. They don't care if you hate your job, your spouse, or even your life. They just want you home for Thanksgiving."

—*Richard Riley, father*

"If anyone gets mad at me for what I do, I just tell them about the Green Hair Theory. It's real, you can look it up. A brilliant hacker came up with it. Anyway, I ask them: 'Did you know you have green hair?' And they laugh and say, 'No, I don't.' I say, 'How do you know?' And they say, ''Cause I just do.'

"And then you say, 'Well, did you know you were a terrible person and other people hate you?' And they say, 'Wait! What are you talking about? What do you mean? Who hates me?' They're upset. They're mad.

"And see, there it is. If people were sure of themselves, if they were positive they weren't bad people, then they wouldn't be upset by what you say. You could call them sluts or whores or thieves or assholes and they'd laugh as hard as they did when you said

their hair was green. They'd totally blow you off.
But they don't. See, they're secretly scared they are
every bad thing you say they are. And it's like they've
been waiting for someone to catch them. Waiting to
be found out for the frauds they are. They're begging
for it.

   "By the way, Tola Riley has green hair."

                              —*Chelsea Patrick, classmate*

VALIDATION

We are in limbo. Because we're still waiting for the school board to make a decision about Mr. Mymer. Because we are slogging through the weeks between Thanksgiving and Christmas break. Because we are slogging from here to eternity.

Outside, the world has turned to gray slush overnight. We don't wear boots to school the way our parents warn us to. *Boots are so lame.* We compensate by layering scarves. Our necks are warm, but our soaked sneakers leave footprints in the hallways, like the markings of ghosts. We slip and we slide on the tile, losing our balance, waving our arms wildly to compensate, the scarves lashing the air. Cell phones skid and shatter.

The kids are still talking about me and about Mr. Mymer, but they're more subdued now, muffled by all the scarves and the cold, which every year catches us by surprise. I look for Chelsea Patrick around every corner—*Who's that tripping over my bridge?* I think she's the one who created The Truth About Tola Riley in the first place. But also I think she's just biding her time.

June waits for me in the cafeteria. She's ditched her mom's cheese sandwich and is dipping a hot dog into a little tub of mayonnaise.

"Gourmet," I say approvingly. I tell her about our mayonnaise project in cooking, and she tells me she likes her mayonnaise "unadulterated."

The NASA phone beeps, and she glances at the screen. "Have you heard about the true story of the three little pigs?"

"Yeah," I say. "The wolf was framed."

"No, actually. Some weird little girl kidnapped all the pigs. Did you get suspended?"

"No. I have to see the school psychologist. And I have to take biology over the summer."

"Could have been worse."

"I don't see how," I say.

"Mr. Anderson could have pickled you with the pigs."

"I think he wanted to."

"Do you blame him? You kidnapped a pig. What's next?"

"I'm plotting my next move."

"You mean you're plotting your own expulsion. Do you want to be thrown out of school?"

"No, I just want them to listen to me. I want them to hear me."

"And you get them to listen by stealing a pig?"

"Think of it as performance art."

"Think of it as C-R-A-Z-Y."

"Everyone already thinks the worst of me. I might as well take advantage of it. I might as well enjoy it," I say.

"Right," she says. "You look like you're having a great time."

She's scooping out a wad of mayo with her finger when a note lands in the middle of our table.

ART TEACHERS DO IT IN SHADES.

"Speaking of ecstasy," I say. "It's for you."

Pete Santorini, Ben Grossman, and Alex Nobody-Can-Pronounce-His-Last-Name gasp when June puts her finger into her mouth and sucks it clean.

"Sorry, boys," she says. "Who needs an art teacher when we've got each other?"

Whoop. Hoot. High five.

"Thanks," I say. "I can imagine the rumors you just started."

June considers me. "What do you care? I thought you were enjoying yourself."

"Not so much. I ran into Chelsea Patrick."

She sighs. "What did she do?"

"Grabbed me and drew a smiley face on my face. With red lipstick."

"I guess it could have been worse. She could have rammed your head into the toilet bowl." She touches her hair as if this has happened to her.

"Are you trying to make me feel better? I know she's the one who started all these rumors. She already ruined my life."

"I don't know," she says. "Mr. Mymer's life seems to be a little more ruined than yours."

"What?"

"Well, you're just a teenager. People might think you're weird or crazy, but no one's going to keep you from going to college or whatever, right? But Mr. Mymer's an adult. And he doesn't have a job."

"Is that what people are saying?"

"Who? What people?"

"The people you're texting?"

"I'm texting some kids from my Youth Leaders of America seminar."

"Because this isn't my fault." Even to me, my voice sounds too high and tight.

"I didn't say it was," she says. "I'm just saying that some people might have it worse, that's all."

The NASA phone rings. She snatches it up. "Hello? What? I didn't call you. You called me. No, *you* called *me*. Yes, you did!" She hangs up.

I use the call as a cue to change the subject. "Seven Chillman came to my house before Thanksgiving."

"He did? What happened?"

"Nothing, really. He found Pib in his backyard and

wanted to bring him home. We talked in my kitchen. Then my mom threw him out."

"Did he kiss you?"

"No. Well, he kissed my hand. But he also asked if we could go to a movie or something."

"He did? Why didn't you text me?"

"Well, it's not like I can actually go. My mom will never let me. I'll be lucky if I can date before I'm thirty-five."

"So sneak."

"I can't do that! She'll ground me."

June laughs. "Tola, your reputation is shot. You just said you kidnapped a pig because you don't care what people think about you. You said it was 'artistic.' What does it even matter what you do now?" She pops the last bit of hot dog into her mouth. "If you really want to be some sort of crazy art rebel, you're going to have to put a lot more work into it."

"I don't want to be a rebel. I just want to be . . ." I don't know how to finish the sentence.

"I think you need to paint something. You get cranky when you're not painting."

"Can't. I need a muse or something. And not an imaginary one. A real one. Someone I can see every day." I'm about to say *someone I can touch*, but the words curl in my mouth.

After school, I go to see the school psychologist for the first time. She's not happy to see me.

● ● ●

At home, the world has begun to pull in on itself. We eat dinner in the dark. Pib moves from window to window, looking for the best view. He sleeps on one of the bookshelves, curled around the clay vase I made my mom in the fifth grade. The furnace drones like a living thing, muffling sounds and words. A thousand times I think I'm going to tell my mom that Madge told me what she did, but it only reminds me what I did. I hover in the doorway: not in this room, not in that room, neither here or there. It takes me a second to recognize the ring of the phone. The number's so new that only a few people know what it is. We hardly ever get any calls.

"HELLO?" Grandma Emmy shouts into the phone no matter how many times you tell her she doesn't have to, like people who write their emails in all capitals.

"Grandma?"

Grandma Emmy doesn't like to use the phone. Though she's had them in her house her whole life, she acts like they are alien things, strange contraptions designed so that telemarketers could interrupt a decent person's dinner and harass her into buying even more contraptions. She says that my cell phone will give me earlobe cancer and makes me put it in the other room when I'm over for dinner. She says that she hates talking on the phone, any phone, hates the way everyone sounds so fake and hollow and small.

Grandma does not sound small. "HELLO? HELLO? WHO'S THIS?"

"Grandma, it's Tola."

"WHO?"

"Tola, Grandma."

"TOLA?"

"Yes, Grandma, it's me. Is everything okay?"

"YES. NO. YES. GET YOUR MOTHER FOR ME."

I run for the living room, where my mother is slumped in her favorite green chair. She's staring off into space, appearing, in my opinion, stupid. Grandma's voice bleats from the handset, "TOLA? ARE YOU THERE?"

My mother snaps out of her trance. She grabs the phone and presses it to her ear. "Mom?" she says. "What's up?"

I hear Grandma shouting on the other end, but I can't make out what she's saying.

"Okay, Mom. I can hear you. Stop yelling. And slow down."

She does. I shift my weight from one foot to the other, waiting. As if she can smell trouble, Madge drifts down the stairs. "What's going on?" she asks me.

"Grandma's on the phone," I say.

"Grandma?" she says, incredulous.

Mom is listening and nodding. "No, of course it was okay to call me. I know everything will be fine, but I'll be right over to make sure." She hands me the receiver. "I have to go to the hospital. Grandpa still isn't feeling well, and you know how Grandma gets. She called an ambulance."

Madge says, "What? What's wrong with him?"

"He's coughing a lot and having some trouble catching his breath," my mom says.

"I knew this was going to happen," Madge says.

"What?" I say. "You knew what was going to happen?"

"He's dying."

My mom's mouth tightens. "No, he's not dying. He's having some trouble catching his breath."

"That sounds like dying," Madge says.

"It sounds like bronchitis," says my mother crisply. "He skipped the doctor's appointment I made, that's all. I don't know why people don't listen to me." She sits up and shoves her feet into her boots. "I'm going to see what's up. I'll be back."

"Should I call the office?" It's Saturday and Mr. Doctor is seeing another boatload of elementary school kids and middle-schoolers. But I'm sure he could reschedule. Mr. Doctor always drives.

"No, don't bother calling. I'm fine."

"Who's going to drive?" I say.

Mom frowns. "I have been driving for more than twenty-five years, you know. Quite successfully."

"I want to come with you," Madge says.

"That's not necessary."

"This is my grandfather we're talking about." Madge's voice saws through the room, the jagged edge of it threatening to cut us to pieces. "I have a right to be there."

"There's no need to be so melodramatic," my mother

says. "He has a cough."

"Just because I *care* about people, just because I have an actual *heart*, doesn't mean I'm melodramatic."

Mom takes a deep breath, the kind you take when you'd really like to flatten someone with a frying pan but remember that's not the best way to show your understanding and concern. "You're right. You can distract your grandmother. She's a little nervous."

They're making me nervous. "I want to come, too."

Mom considers this. "Tola, I really don't think this is an emergency," she says, glancing askance at my sister. "Your grandpa will be fine. Really."

"If Madge is going, then I'm going."

"Her name is Tiffany."

"Whatever."

At the hospital, we stop at the emergency room. I was there once six years ago when Madge broke her wrist while running backward (she claimed I talked her into doing it). I remember being so bored that I sneaked past the nurses at the nurses' station and into the treatment area. I watched a teenager, a boy, beaten and bloody, getting his head stitched up like Frankenstein's monster until one of the orderlies noticed me.

This time, we're told that Grandpa Joe has been admitted, so we have to go around to the regular part of the hospital to find him. On our way, we stop in the cafeteria to get sodas, and then we stop at the gift shop to get balloons. Then we take the elevator to the eighth floor.

I thought that the regular floors would look different from the emergency room, that they would look the way they look on TV, sterile and bustling with tortured but brilliant doctors running around with defibrillators or maybe freshly baked goods given to them by the families of grateful patients pulled back from the brink of death. No one warned me about the smell, which is a combination of alcohol, piss, and gravy. No one told me about the half-dressed old people slumped in wheelchairs in the hallways or the visitors with pinched faces and tears in their eyes at the nurses' station.

I don't like this place.

Neither does Grandpa Joe.

"Tell me you're here to spring me from the slammer," he says as soon as he sees us.

"Hi, Dad," my mom says. "How are you feeling?"

"Did you bring the pie with the file inside?"

"We brought balloons!" says my mom way too cheerfully. The balloons are tied to a weighted teddy bear that she plunks on the bedside table.

"I guess that means no," he says.

"Hi, Grandpa!" I say, also way too cheerfully, because I can't stand the alcohol–piss–gravy smell.

"You're a sight for sore eyes," Grandpa says when Madge and I kiss him. His cheek is pale and papery. He's in a hospital gown that exposes stringy arms. An IV pumps drugs or fluid or whatever into him, and he's got clear tubes up his nose for oxygen. Grandma Emmy is sitting on the chair in the corner. The chair is so big that it looks like it's trying to swallow her. She gets up so that we can dump our coats and hats on it.

A guy comes in the room. He looks like my history teacher. Except he says he's a doctor. He points to his name tag with the little *M.D.* on it, as if that proves anything. He tells us that my grandpa has some pneumonia in one lung and he needs antibiotics to get rid of it. Because of his age, they're going to watch him closely.

"Hey," says Grandpa Joe. "Watch what you say about my age."

The young guy grabs my grandpa's foot. "Ha ha," he says. I don't think the doctors should go around grabbing people's feet. I want to tell him that, but he walks out before I can.

"See," my mom says. "The doctor says Grandpa Joe is going to be fine." I'm not sure who she's talking to. Maybe all of us. Maybe herself. "Tiffany, did you hear what the doctor said? Just a few days and he'll be out of here."

Madge folds her arms across her chest and clamps her mouth shut.

Grandpa Emmy tucks the blankets tighter around Grandpa. "That was a doctor? How old was he? Seventeen?"

"Oh, he was at least nineteen," my mom says. I think he looked about forty, but nobody's asking for my opinion.

"How's your breathing feel now, Dad?" my mom says.

Grandpa Joe shrugs. "Better. A little better. Still tight in there, though." He pats his chest.

Madge unclamps her mouth. "I know how that feels."

"Tiffany," says Mom.

"What?"

"Be quiet."

"What?" says Madge. "What did I say?"

"We're here for Grandpa Joe."

"I *know* that."

Grandma Emmy snaps, "Anita, why are you so angry all the time? Maybe you should stop drinking coffee."

Mom glances at me and jerks her head toward the door. I get the hint. "Madge, let's go get a snack. I'm hungry."

"When *aren't* you hungry?" But she doesn't argue. She follows me out the door. We get on the elevator. She presses 2 for the cafeteria. At 4, the doors open. There's nobody waiting but a boy about ten shuffles down the hallway, dragging an IV. His head is shaved, and he has a red scar above his ear. We see the bright glint of the staples holding the wound closed. The boy says, "What are you staring at?"

"What?" says Madge. "We're not staring. We're going down."

"So go," the boy says.

I punch 2 again and the doors start to close. "Bye," I say, waving. He rolls his eyes.

"He was rude," Madge whispers. "Why was he so rude?"

"He has staples in his head," I say. "You'd be rude, too."

"Apart from the staples, he looked okay. I mean, I bet there are cancer kids here. People dying. Like Grandpa."

"The doctor said he was going to be fine," I say.

"Shows what he knows," Madge says.

There's a story my grandpa likes to tell over dinner, a story about my sister, Tiffany, before she became the Madge we all know and love and occasionally want to bury in the backyard. When she was very small, not even four, she and Grandpa were eating peanut butter sandwiches at the park. The way Grandpa tells it, she looked at Grandpa very seriously and solemnly over the crust of her sandwich, and said, "Why are you so old?"

Grandpa answered, "Because I was born a long time ago."

"Can't somebody fix it?"

"Honey, I wish they could."

As much as Madge loves Grandpa, I think it might be easier for her if he were suffering with something more life-threatening, more cinematic—a bear attack, a war wound stapled shut, a fall down a well. She needs the validation.

(*comments*)

"We talk every day, but there's a lot she doesn't tell me. Sometimes I try to ask her questions about it, but she only answers the ones she wants to answer, and if you push her, she'll change the subject. I think that she does that to herself, too. In her own head. Skips things. Changes the subject. She forgets so much, or remembers only the way she wants to. Like the time we kissed in the art room. She always says it was my idea. It wasn't. It was hers.

"I think that maybe something did happen with Mr. Mymer. But don't tell her I said that, okay?"

—*June Leon, classmate*

"People always want to know where my name came from. But if I explain it, they feel sorry for me. And who needs that?

"The truth: I was found in a park when I was three. The woman who found me and brought me to the police said she'd seen a man leave me under the slide.

A white guy. Tall. Skinny. Wearing running shorts with shiny dress shoes, like he was going to a fancy dinner and forgot to put on his suit. She said he came out of the woods with me, left me, and disappeared into the woods again. It's in the police report. I don't remember any of it. The guy never came forward, and the police never found him. I was put into foster care. My parents took me in when I was four, then adopted me when I was seven. My brother said that I act like my life began when I was seven, so he started calling me Seven. He thinks it's some kind of insult, but I like it. People are more curious about my nickname than they are about my adoption. And hardly anyone guesses I'm adopted because I'm the same shade of brown as the rest of my family. People say I look like my brother. If you want to piss my brother off, just tell him that.

"Listen, my parents are my parents and my brother is my brother and that's good enough for me. I feel bad for the skinny guy who left me in the park. That doesn't make me some great person or anything. Just a smart one. Love the people who love you back."

—*Seven Chillman, classmate*

"Joe is sick. Nothing else matters anymore. Joe's sick, and everything's changed."

—*Emmeline King, maternal grandmother*

THREES

After Grandpa goes to the hospital, the Earth seems content to twirl its lazy way around and around, oblivious to both our happiness and our misery.

Then three things happen.

1.

I shuffle into the kitchen one morning to find my mother handing Madge some sort of pill from a big brown bottle. "What's that?" I say. "Do you have a fever?"

Madge bursts into noisy sobs, startling Mr. Doctor so much that he sloshes milk over the side of his cereal bowl. "Can't you mind your own business?" Madge shrieks. "Do you have to know everything about everybody? I have a headache, okay?"

"Okay, okay!"

"What are you going to do? Paint it in one of your stupid pictures?"

"Why would I paint a picture of your headache? Actually, *how* would I do that?"

As soon as I say it, I see it, a portrait of Madge in a forest so deep green it's almost black, kneeling with her head on a wooden chopping block, with the robber bridegroom—the character from *Grimm's* who convinces young girls to marry him and then kills and eats them—standing over her with an ax. Even though Mr. Mymer was always saying that these flashes of inspiration we believe are so brilliant are often clichés we've seen a million times before, I think it's a fabulous idea. I want to ask Madge to sit for me, but she runs from the room. Pib runs after her. My mother sighs.

"What? What did I say?"

"Nothing," says my mom. "It was just a vitamin anyway."

But, later, when I steal a glance at the label on the bottle, it says *fluoxetine*, which Google tells me is the generic name for Prozac.

2.

When I open my locker before class, there's a pink cupcake sitting on the top shelf. On it is the number 7. It is delicious.

3.

At lunch, June comes running over, waving the NASA phone. "It's done. The board issued a press release. They decided that there was no evidence. Mymer's coming back."

(*comments*)

"I don't get to see her much. We have opposite schedules; our classes are in different wings of the school. But I hid around the corner to watch her find the cupcake. June gave me the combination to the locker. I've been experimenting with different ingredients. This one was coconut with a cream-cheese icing. I put a dash of almond in the batter.

"Anyway, when she found it, the first thing she did was smell it. Then she took a huge bite. She got icing all over her face. I think that's why I like her. For the good stuff, she's willing to get icing all over her face. Who wouldn't want a girl like that?"

—*Seven Chillman, classmate*

"If the drugs kill me, blame it on my mother and that bloody therapist."

—*Tiffany Riley, sister*

LIAR

The school is abuzz, aflame, afire with the news of Mr. Mymer's return. For a few minutes, I think: *It's over! It's done! I'm free!*

Until I am asked the same questions I was asked a month ago: Is Mr. Mymer going to leave his wife for you? Are you getting married? What kind of dress will you wear to the wedding? Are you going to have his baby?

The real story doesn't matter to anyone. They're only interested in the story that they helped to tell. But I don't care. They can say what they want. Mr. Mymer's coming back.

I'm sitting in health class as we're going over our CPR skills. Ms. Rothschild suddenly doubles over at her desk. As Ms. Rothschild has been pregnant about a thousand years and is as big as three people, this is a little worrisome. We're certain that a litter of puppies is imminent.

"Are you okay? Are you going to puke?" Heather and/or Feather Whitestone wants to know.

"Um," says Ms. Rothschild. "I think my water just broke."

"What does *that* mean?" demands Tim Corcoran.

"It means that someone should go get the principal before this class turns into a live demonstration."

Tim bolts from his seat as if his life depends on it. Ms. Rothschild continues to huff and pant in the most unlady-like way. Heather/Feather keeps asking if she's going to puke until Ms. Rothschild tells her to jump off a bridge. A comment that Heather/Feather seems to find unnecessarily hostile. The principal gets there in about five minutes, saying he's called an ambulance. He ushers the students out into the hallway and has us join the gym class already in progress.

The good news: Seven Chillman is in the gym class.

The bad news: We are forced to play paddleball. Anyone wearing a dress is excused from the activities. Since I'm wearing leggings under my dress, I'm not excused.

Paddleball, if you're not familiar, is a version of racquetball played with oversized Ping-Pong paddles. I'm not allowed to play with Seven. Today, it's my job to count how many times John Jarmen, state tennis champion and resident ass, can hit the ball against the wall in a minute for one of those stupid skills tests Mr. Hoosbacher, the gym teacher, is so fond of.

John smiles his super white smile at me and says, "Hope you can count fast." I force a laugh. Everyone laughs at John Jarmen's jokes. Not because they're funny, but because he's six foot three and because last year he pounded a French exchange student named Etienne, who made the mistake of sitting at his table in the cafeteria.

Anyway, John drops the blue ball on the ground, swings his arm, and slams the ball . . .

. . . right into a crack in the cinderblock wall.

Both of us watch as the ball ricochets off the crack and goes whizzing across the gym. John is so surprised that he just stands there, waiting for the ball to come back and apologize. Then he shakes his head and dashes after it, but he gets stuck dodging the other balls (think enraged giraffe trying to negotiate an obstacle course). When he finally makes it back to our court, Mr. Hoosbacher yells, "Time!"

Mr. Hoosbacher walks to each counter with his clipboard, asking for the numbers so that he could record them. "How many?"

"One."

"You lie!" says John.

I'm so surprised I don't say anything for a minute. Then I say, "Your first ball hit the crack in the wall."

"So?"

"So," I answer slowly, as if talking to a non-English speaker, "you didn't make it back to the court in time to hit any other balls. You got one hit."

"You lie!" he says again. I wait for him to say something else, to explain himself, but he doesn't. I realize that he's waiting for *me* to say something else. And some other day, before all of this, maybe I would have. Maybe I would have made up a number: fifty-seven-point-nine—nine-two-five-eight and a half. Maybe I would have claimed a giant butterfly with a lion's head flew into the room and I couldn't see for all those gossamer wings and whiskery catness. Maybe I would have said a team of hacky-sack-playing leprechauns distracted me. Maybe I would have claimed that paddleball is not a real sport and that I refused to participate in skills tests out of principle. Maybe, to keep things simple, I would have just appeared stupid.

Now, everything's different. My favorite teacher was almost fired. My grandfather is sick. I almost watched a live birth, something I don't plan on watching even if I'm the one actually giving birth.

I am way too tired for this crap.

I say, "You got one hit."

"Bitch," he says. "You're a lying little bitch."

"Hey! Watch the mouth, Jarmen!" says Mr. Hoosbacher. "And relax! It's one skills test. No big deal."

"She's lying," John says. He has beads of sweat on his forehead.

"Yeah?" says Mr. Hoosbacher. "Why would she do that?"

"How the hell should I know?"

"What did I say about the mouth?" Mr. Hoosbacher marks a red *1* next to John Jarmen's name. "Next time, pay more attention to ball placement," he says, and wanders over to the next court, where the Whitestone sisters are arguing about who is skinnier.

John Jarmen watches him walk away. "Freak."

"Original," I say. He's got more than a foot and a hundred pounds on me. He could use me to stir his drinks. It's clear my mother is right and I need some sort of professional help, because I can't seem to help myself.

"You look like a boy," he says. "I can't believe Mymer went for you. I can't believe anyone would go for you."

I think about Etienne, who, after having his two front teeth neatly punched from his jaw, put both his hands on his hips and said in that nasally way that made him sound constantly annoyed: "How did you do that for?"

I hold out my hand. "My turn."

"What?"

"It's my turn," I say. "Give me the paddle."

"I'll give you the paddle," he say. "I'd love to give you the paddle."

"Okay," I say, and snatch it right out of his hand. I guess I didn't think he would do anything to me when I grabbed for it, but I should have taken into consideration the terrible athletic disappointment he'd just suffered, because he reaches out, puts his hand *over my face*, and shoves. I land on my butt, hard, and skid across the polished floor like a human hockey puck.

He looks down at me. "You can keep the paddle," he says, and then he turns and struts over to the Whitestone twins, who are trying very hard not to giggle and are failing.

Before I even know what I'm going to do, I get up off the floor and run up behind him. The twins' giggles change to bleats of surprise when I whack John Jarmen as hard as I can on his big bubble butt. There's a crack, then a burst of pointillated light, like Georges Seurat took over the universe, tossing his fractured fairy dust in my eyes.

It's snowing stars. The ceiling now looks a rich, deep blue, the color a little kid paints the ocean. The wood floors are gone, replaced by a vast field of white flowers. I can feel the stems poking into my back. I can smell the blooms. They smell like sugar and cinnamon. My mouth waters.

Someone walks toward me. He wears pants that stop short at the knee, a gold shirt that shimmers in the fairy-dusted air, and a green velvet cape that sweeps behind him. The ruby set in the center of his crown winks. As he gets closer, I see his eyes, silver as sun on water. He kneels and holds out his hand.

"Are you all right?" he says.

I have a hard time finding my voice. I've misplaced it somewhere in my body; it's hiding in an ankle or an elbow or a kidney.

Finally, I croak, "Who are you?"

"Me?" He seems surprised I don't recognize him. But I do. I think. But he's so different. Different and the same.

He presses a palm to his chest and bows his head slightly. "I'm Prince Charming."

"Prince Charming is a brown dude?"

"Obviously."

"You should sue Disney."

He pats me on the head and then looks away. "Did you see anyone run by? A princess maybe? Missing a shoe?"

"No."

"Are you sure?"

"Well, no."

"It would be better if you're sure."

"I'm sure it would be better if I was sure, but I'm not sure."

He shakes his head. "And I guess you don't wear shoes."

"What? Why would you think that?"

"Because," he says, pointing to my feet.

I look down. Sprouting from the ends of my shins are the marmalade-colored claws of a bird.

The stars fade. I feel hands gripping my shoulders. Jewels gleam back at me. Bright gray jewels set in a brown face.

Seven says, "Are you all right?"

"It's you!" I say.

Seven smiles. "Yes, it's me."

Mr. Hoosbacher shoves Seven aside. "Tola Riley!" he booms. He claps his ham hands as if he's trying to get the attention of a deaf dog. "Can you hear me?"

"Russians in space can hear you, Mr. Hoosbacher," I say. I glance past him and see everyone standing around, their faces floating over me like balloons. I blink at the balloon heads and try to get up.

"Lie still." I don't know who says this, but it's extremely annoying. I don't like to be told what to do. I stagger to my feet. The balloon heads part, and I see that Mr. Hoosbacher has pulled John Jarmen aside and is now waving his arms wildly and shouting. The phrases "overgrown mountain troll" and "expelled from the planet" echo through the gym.

"What happened?" I say.

"You were looking right at me," Seven says, "but you seemed really out of it."

"I *was* out of it. But what I meant was, why was I lying on the ground in the first place?"

"The troll punched you," Seven says. "You don't remember?"

"I've never been punched before," I say. "I always wondered if I could take it."

He blinks his silver eyes. "Is that why you paddled him? To see if he'd punch you?"

"No," I say. "I paddled him because he's a troll. And I'm tired of all the bloody trolls. They ruin everything."

"That chick is crazy," says one of the balloon heads. "She's some kind of deranged munchkin."

"Yeah," says another balloon head. "Munchkin. From, like, Munchkin Land."

"*Psycho* Munchkin Land."

"Better watch it," Seven says. "She's got a badminton

racket with your name on it."

I smile at Seven.

He smiles back.

"I think I need to go to the nurse."

Seven reaches out and takes my arm. "That's a good idea. I'll walk you there."

But this is not to be. Mr. Hoosbacher takes me to the nurse himself, and the nurse calls the principal, the principal calls the school psychologist, and the psychologist calls my mom. The psychologist makes the nurse get rid of the three kids faking fevers and stomachaches and drags a chair over to sit down next to me.

"How are you, Tola?"

"I really wish you hadn't called my mom."

"You've been hurt by another student. We had to inform her."

"I'm fine."

"I'm sure you're fine, but we need to cover our bases."

Cover your butts, you mean. "Now she's going to make me get a CAT scan."

"Is that such a bad thing?"

"She'll assume that it's my fault."

"John Jarmen was suspended."

"For how many years?"

"I don't think your mom will be angry. She'll be concerned."

"Anger, concern, it's all the same to her."

The psychologist takes off her glasses. Her hands are shaking. This does not inspire confidence.

"Are you having problems at home, Tola? With your mom, maybe?"

"You've never had problems with your mom?"

"Maybe a few."

"Okay, then."

"A long time ago."

"When you were my age?"

She purses her lips. "Yes."

"See? Even people who eventually become professional educators have problems with their parents."

She takes a tissue from her pocket and vigorously rubs lint into her glasses. "What about your dad?"

"I haven't seen him in a couple of months. He just got married."

"And are you upset about that?"

"Not particularly. I don't like his wife."

"That must be hard."

"Not as hard as living with one kidney."

"Oh! When did you lose your kidney?"

"I didn't."

She blinks as if she's just run into a cloud of gnats and wipes the lenses that much harder. "The reason why I asked about your parents is because sometimes, when we're unhappy, we do things that we think will make us feel better. Like, say, paddling John Jarmen. Though I have to admit you wouldn't be the first student to want to hit him."

"John Jarmen put his hand over my face and pushed me to the floor. He deserved to be paddled. I don't feel bad about it. I feel good. Even though he punched me afterward. I can take a punch."

"I know. You've been taking a lot of them." She pauses. It is a Significant Pause. I think they teach those in therapy school. "You were close to Mr. Mymer."

"Yes, but not in the way everyone thinks."

"Why don't you set me straight?"

"You won't believe me," I say.

"Why not?"

"Nobody does."

"The school board does. The police do. Tell me about Mr. Mymer."

"He's a good teacher."

"What makes him good?"

"He thinks art is important."

"And other people don't."

"If other people thought art was important, then it would be required to graduate. But no, I don't have to take art. I do have to take math, which is just a waste of time because the numbers get all switched up in my brain, plus, calculators exist for a reason. I do have to take history, which is basically memorizing tariff acts till your brain bleeds. I *do* have to take four years of gym class with a bunch of jerks who punch me if they don't like what I say. But art? Optional. Even though art and music and literature and all that are what make us human. Algebra doesn't make us human. Games don't make us human."

She smiles. "Well. You're certainly passionate about all this."

I sit up. "Is *passionate* another word for crazy?"

"Of course not," she says.

For a brief second, I'm hopeful. Then she ruins it. "But it might help you to start talking to people." I start to protest, but she puts up her hand. "I mean *really* talking. No snarky comments. No snide remarks. No kidnapping pigs. No fairy tales." She puts her glasses back on. "We care about you. We'd love to hear what you want to say, whenever you want to say it. We'd like to know what the real story is. Your story."

The psychologist is still nervous and sort of fragile, like if I cried, she'd cry, too. And she's wearing one of those cheap suits that looks both itchy and flammable. I feel bad for her. So I tell her about my cat. My grandpa Joe. The little houses my dad used to make for us. Weird stories from *Grimm's* like the one about a poor fisherman who gets a bunch of wishes granted by an enchanted flounder. My painting. She asks me to sketch something for her, so I do.

But the whole time I'm sketching, I'm thinking about Mr. Mymer, how easy he was to talk to, how you didn't have to feel bad for him to want to tell him things. I'm imagining the art room at lunchtime, how good it smelled, how safe it felt. How he asked me about my name and I told him it could have been anything. Christina. Ashley. Katie. But no, in a fit of generosity that she would never again repeat, my mother let my father name me, and he chose Cenerentola. CHE-NER-EN-TOLA. Dad said he got the name from his favorite opera, *La Cenerentola*, but I don't buy it. He liked Cenerentola because it's another name for Cinderella, but he didn't want to admit it. And he never really had a favorite opera; the opera thing was just a phase he was going through around the time I was born, something to take his mind off the fact that he wasn't making any money. A month later, my mom said, he'd taken up tai chi and forgotten about it.

In the *Grimm's* version of "Cinderella," I told Mr. Mymer, the girl's name is Aschenputtel. I suppose I should be glad that I'm not walking around with *that* on my report card.

And then, the other times, I told Mr. Mymer how my dad left my mom for the Hound from Hell and my mom turned into one of those helicopter parents almost overnight, hovering noisily overhead as if me and Madge might spontaneously combust and die if she wasn't around to hose us off. Though, I said, in Madge's case that might be true. I remember him asking what my family was like before the divorce, and I told him that I remember my mom working a lot, her tendency to be sarcastic at the most inconvenient times—as in all the time—and my dad sculpting all night and getting gloomy and impossible when he couldn't sell anything. I remember months of fighting, years of it, and then a glacial silence that was somehow worse, a silence that muffled us all, so that the simple act of asking for the salt at dinner became painful and misunderstood.

But then I told him that memories are Madge's department, that my own memories are usually too fuzzy to be of much use, and I could be making up the fighting and the glacial silences. (I read lots of teen novels, mostly before I became an actual teen, and maybe my brain's been infiltrated with ideas not my own. Really, I said, why else would I use the word *glacial*?) But Madge, well, Madge is the elephant of the family. I told Mr. Mymer that Madge liked to whip out some horrible thing she insisted you said or did in the car on the way to see the Statue of Liberty, and though you *know* you couldn't possibly be the kind of person to have said or have done such a terrible thing, you can't argue with her because you don't even remember going to the Statue of Liberty, not ever in your whole life, and even if you had, you must have been six years old at the most, and what six-year-old hasn't said something horrible to her older sister? I told him that she does it to Mom, too, and it drove Mom crazy because she couldn't remember, either.

And I remember Mr. Mymer saying this: "Maybe Madge's memories aren't as accurate as you all believe."

"Why wouldn't they be?" I said.

"Well, you said she seemed depressed; kind of gloomy

like your dad. Sometimes depressed people see the world differently."

"Maybe they see it for what it really is."

"What is it?"

"Crap."

The bell rings and I'm still sitting with the fragile, flammable psychologist. She tells me how happy she is that I've opened up to her. That she feels we can work together and make progress. She thanks me for the sketch—the enchanted flounder—which she likes enough to keep for her office.

She means well, so I don't tell her that it's easy to sound like you're being personal when you're not. That a professional should be able to tell the difference. And that if I really wanted to open up, I'd confess that I really am the liar everyone believes I am.

(*comments*)

"I wasn't too confident how our meetings would go after that disastrous conference about the pignapping. And I'd heard from others how guarded she was. I was happy to be wrong. We discussed her feelings for Mr. Mymer, her feelings about her parents. I got a lot of good background. I think she's a very confused young girl, but I have a hard time believing that anything untoward happened with her art teacher. I think her behavior has a lot more to do with her family of origin. In future sessions, I'd like to explore her relationship with her father."

—*Diane Word, psychologist*

"What kills me is that she called me that day. She wanted to have lunch."

—*Richard Riley, father*

SILENCE IS GOLDEN, DUCT TAPE IS SILVER

Once upon a time, there was a girl. Though she was not a particularly bad girl—nor a particularly good one—most people found her a little strange. Often this made her sad, but not always. She liked to be alone (or so she told herself).

One day, her favorite teacher gives her a task. Not impossible—no separating lentils from piles of ashes, spinning straw into gold. All she's supposed to do is visit a museum and write a journal entry about it. The teacher hands out lists of local galleries and places in New York City to choose from. "No showing is too big or small," he says.

The girl picks a museum in New York City. This is the city where her father lives with his new wife. The father's new wife doesn't like the girl. When the girl calls her father's apartment and asks if he would meet her for lunch, the stepmother claims he's far too busy and that he'd have to see the girl another time. If it were up to the stepmother, the girl thinks, she would never see her own father again. The girl wonders about women like her stepmother. How they can look themselves in the mirror. Then she remembers that women like her stepmother enjoy looking in mirrors.

Still, even without the prospect of seeing her father, the girl is excited. It is late September, and the city is enjoying one last gasp of summer. When she arrives on the bus, the trees are just turning red and yellow, and the people are walking around in thin scarves and gauzy skirts whipped up by warm breezes and burnished by the golden sunlight. The city itself looks like a magnificent painting.

She gets to the museum and goes directly to the Georges-Pierre Seurat exhibit. She examines not his paintings but his drawings, made of lots of tiny dots. She likes dots. She reaches out to touch one of the drawings, and a guard yells at her.

After she views the drawings, she decides to go to the cafeteria for a snack. She finds a table in a deserted corner, half hidden by a large sandwich-board menu. She sits alone, scribbling notes in her journal, adding little sketches here and there. Her stomach rumbles, so she goes to the counter to order some food and is told a waitress will bring it. When she returns to her table, she thinks about the artist and the wonders he created. But mostly she's thinking about how all the other tables in the café are filled with two or more people. She ponders the wonder of *that*, of two people finding each other and going to a museum to admire the art. The girl had tried to get a friend to come with her and couldn't. She'd tried to get her sister to come and couldn't. Her father was busy. Always busy.

The girl imagines what the people are talking about. Some of the people are laughing. A man and a woman lean in toward each other, sharing a piece of pie.

Someone clears his throat. She looks up to see her favorite teacher standing above her, a study in browns and oranges, his pumpkin-colored hair sticking up in every direction. His T-shirt says: SILENCE IS GOLDEN, DUCT TAPE IS SILVER.

"Hello, Ms. Riley," he says. "Fancy meeting you here." His voice is surprisingly low for someone so skinny.

"Hey, Mr. Mymer." She has never seen this teacher outside a school setting before, and it makes her confused and nervous. She forgets that teachers are actually people and not avatars that come preloaded with the classrooms, the way she sometimes imagines them to be. She wonders how she's supposed to act.

The teacher smiles widely.

Another thing the girl ponders: whitening strips.

But she remembers how much she loves this teacher. And, even more than that, how alone she's been feeling. "How are you?" she says.

"Great, great," Mr. Mymer says. "Which exhibit did you catch?"

"Georges Seurat."

"That's what I came to see," he says. "Incredible, wasn't it? I think I prefer his drawings to his paintings."

"Me too."

A waitress brings the girl's food: a plate of desserts and a hot chocolate. The teacher points at the plate.

"That's a lot of food for one person."

People are often surprised at how much the girl eats. They don't understand how hungry she is.

"This is all for me," she says, and pops a cookie into her mouth. "But I'll share."

"No, thank you." The teacher hesitates a minute, then says, "I'll sit for a sec if you don't mind." He drops his man-purse to the floor and slumps in the chair across from the girl. He places a book, *The World of Gustav Klimt*, on the table. The girl knows the painting on the cover. It is a famous painting called *The Kiss*.

"I don't know why I'm so tired," the teacher says.

"All this art sucks the brains right out of you."

"Probably."

"I meant that in a good way."

"I know. Have you started Friday's sketch assignment?"

"Yeah," she says. "At first, I was just going to do a self-portrait, but then I had this really cool dream. I was in this castle, I think. All stone and stained glass and tapestries. And there was a beautiful queen on the throne. She had the long hair, the blue velvet dress, the birds singing happy songs overhead, all that. The only weird thing was her feet. She didn't have human feet. She had bird's feet. And they were orange."

"Cool."

"If you think about it, the bird's feet make total sense. In the original 'Cinderella,' there were no fairy godmothers or pumpkins or mice. It was a pair of magical birds that gave her the gown and the shoes. They also pecked out the eyes of the wicked stepsisters, but I think I'll spare everyone that part."

"I like it. Though I have to say I'm not surprised." He taps the paperback collection of *Grimm's Fairy Tales* that's sitting on the table. It had once belonged to the girl's father. She carries it everywhere with her.

"People forget how grim fairy tales are. I like to remind them," she says.

"I know."

"I worry sometimes that people won't think that it's art, though. That my subjects belong in cartoons or illustrations."

"Dalí painted melting clocks. I suppose if he'd asked around first, quizzed people if they wanted to see a picture of a melting clock, the answer might have been something obvious, like 'Clocks don't melt!' But, lucky for us, Salvador didn't care what anyone else thought. You use what moves you." The man has said this before. The girl has to wonder if he got it from a T-shirt.

"Still," she says. "It's not like people are wowed by what I do. A lot of times, nobody seems to get it."

"Don't fish for compliments," the teacher replies.

The girl is stung, but she tries not to show it. "How else would I ever get any?"

"Some people understand what you're trying to say with your art. And the rest, well, they'll come around. Or they won't. And maybe you shouldn't care so much." He flips through his book. "I was reading about Gustav Klimt—he was influenced by Seurat and Van Gogh, you know—and I found this. It's called *Nuda Veritas*. The woman is holding up the mirror of truth while the snake of falsehood is dead at her feet. The quote above the figure is this: 'If you cannot please everyone with your deeds and your art, please a few. To please many is bad.'"

The girl looks at the picture. The woman in it is naked. She has red hair with flowers entwined and the kind of thick, white thighs that would be considered fat now. If she were an actress, the studio executives would make her get liposuction.

The girl wonders if her teacher likes girls with red hair and thick thighs, and then chides herself for thinking such stupid things, things only a baby would think.

In her teacher's classroom, she feels old. Outside of it, she feels young. She wants this to be the other way around—she wants to feel older all the time—but she doesn't know how to change it.

"Here," he says. "You can borrow the book if you want. You'll like Klimt's colors at least, even if you don't like his work."

She takes the book, though she doesn't know how it will help. He seems like he's trying to comfort her, to get her to not worry about what people think. But she doesn't know how you stop worrying about what other people think. Especially about her art. Even though she paints scenes from fairy tales, it's the only time she says anything real.

"You said yourself that art is communication," she says. "I don't want to feel like I'm talking to myself."

"So you're unappreciated in your own lifetime. So was Modigliani."

"Modigliani died of meningitis and drug abuse."

"You forgot the misery and the poverty," he says, grinning his yellow grin.

"Always looking on the bright side," she tells him. Her stomach growls, and she slaps an arm over it as if to silence herself.

"You should eat," he says.

"I am." She takes another cookie. It is small, and she devours it whole. As she does this, he pulls the menu from behind the napkin holder and reads it. His hands, she decides, are his best feature. Even better than his eyes, which are big and blue, movie-star eyes. But they are set in an ordinary face, a face with thin lips and a strange black mole that does not look healthy. The hands, though, are something. The year before, they had studied sculpture, spending a long time on Michelangelo's *David*. *David* was perfectly proportioned except for his hands. They were huge. You could see every detail down to the fingernails. But they were beautiful. Large and veined and strong. The imperfection made *David* more perfect.

The teacher has hands like that. Too big for his skinny arms. The girl isn't so good at hands—they're so hard to get right, the reason, she suspects, that even Michelangelo had a tough time—but she wants to paint the teacher's. She wants to touch them.

This is not the first time she's had such thoughts. She's a daydreamer, and sometimes the daydreams take all sorts of twists and turns. In the dreams, she's held the hands. She's touched the face and the pumpkin-colored hair. The black mole has disappeared. The thin lips don't feel as thin, and they taste like lemon tea.

Now, she feels a weird sort of bloom in her stomach. Not hunger, exactly, though it's a little like hunger. The bloom spreads until it warms her whole body. She glances around nervously. She shifts in her seat, making it creak. She's sure everyone can tell by looking at her.

But then, she is in a strange city. No one knows her here. They don't know where she comes from or how old she is. They don't care. To these people, there's nothing here to see except the art.

The teacher doesn't notice the bloom, the wanting. He's drooling over all the desserts. "These look so good," he says. "Maybe I'll have a little something after all."

He reaches out. She thinks, what could happen? Who

would know? Who would tell?

She grabs his hand before he grabs a cookie. "Now don't think this means I'm trying to trade cookies for grades. I wouldn't want you getting any ideas." His skin is warm, but his fingertips are slightly rough, like cats' tongues. She slides a thumb down the inside of his wrist—so soft!—feeling for the pulse.

"Tola," he says. He gently pulls his hand from hers. "Teachers aren't allowed to have ideas." He stands and gathers his bag, forgetting *The Kiss* between them.

After he has walked away, the girl hears a strange sort of snorting laugh from across the cafeteria. She knows that laugh.

But when the girl turns to look, the other one is gone.

(comments)

"I was there to see the art, same as anyone. I just happened to be walking by the café when I saw them. The look on her face. Holy crap, she was desperate. I mean, I'll-do-anything-for-you-if-you-please-love-me desperate. Pathetic. And then she tries to hold his hand. I laughed out loud, and then I had to duck behind a group of Japanese tourists so she didn't see me.

"And Mymer? Never liked that guy. His dumb hair and his stupid T-shirts. Who the hell does he think he is?

"Oh yeah. Fired."

—Chelsea Patrick, classmate

SCREAMO

The doctors keep saying that the drugs they used to fix Grandpa's pneumonia have side effects like loss of appetite and diarrhea, that this happens to lots of old people, and that he'll get better soon. Every time we come to the hospital, we expect to find him sitting up in bed, cracking jokes, slurping chocolate pudding, teasing the nurses. But when we visit, he's barely able to keep his eyes open, and we can't get him to eat. We crowd into the room—me, my mom, Madge, Mr. Doctor, Grandma Emmy—our faces screwed up with hope and then worry. We bounce around like atomic particles, bumping into the IV pole and one another. Madge starts glaring, and Mom starts ranting about incompetent doctors, and Grandma Emmy starts wringing her hands and saying maybe we should let him sleep. *Look at him. He's tired. He just wants to sleep. Let him sleep.*

So we let him sleep. Normally, people seem so peaceful

when they sleep, but Grandpa is *too* peaceful. I perch on the end of my seat, watching his chest go up and down, occasionally putting my hand on his bony rib cage to feel the heart fluttering like a bird with a broken wing. He hasn't bothered to put his false teeth in for days—his mouth is all caved in. His breath comes in pants, as if he's dreaming about something that scares him.

What scares me:

1. Grandpa's roommate, ancient and hairless, his two broken ankles in casts, muttering "Babydollbaby-dollbabydollbabydoll" under his breath. When the nurses come to change his sheets, he screams as if they are killing him.

2. A white-haired woman in a wheelchair out in the hallway yelling, "Don't touch me, I hate you! You lie you lie you all lie!" The man who wheels the woman around is her son, his face carefully ironed to a blank.

3. The nurse, a woman with hot pink fingernails and teased blond hair straight out of the eighties, always talking about the squirrels digging up her yard and how she tried to talk her cop husband into shooting them all. The stray cats, too. *Dirty animals.*

Mom can't take it. She drags Mr. Doctor to the nursing station and is threatening lawsuits against the hospital. Grandma Emmy is down in the cafeteria playing cards with

Madge, but I know Grandma's heart can't be in it. She's not losing money. She's just losing.

I sit alone with Grandpa Joe, wondering what to do. I want to tell Grandpa Joe that I keep forgetting to call Dad but that he seems to have forgotten about me, too. I want to tell him that I never lied about what Mr. Mymer did; I just lied about what *I* did, and I didn't really do that much anyway, and now it's all blown out of proportion. And I want to tell him that even good people do stupid things and don't tell the whole story later. Exhibit: Mom and Mr. Rosentople.

But I don't say any of these things. Grandpa can't even put in his own teeth; he can't even get up to use the bathroom. The guy next door is muttering under his breath: "Babydollbabydollbabydollbabydoll." Grandpa breathes in and out, in and out, like some mixed-up version of Sleeping Beauty. I wonder if I should tell him a story. I wonder if he can hear me in his sleep. Madge says that even people in comas respond to the voices of their wives and children and brothers and sisters, so why not Grandpa, who is only sleeping? I try to think of a good story, an uplifting story, but what pops into my head is all wrong. Like the story "The Death of the Little Hen." When Little Hen chokes on a nut, her rooster husband asks every animal in the forest for help, but it all ends in disaster and everyone dies, including the rooster, who has just enough time to bury the little hen before keeling over on top of the grave and dying, too. Or the Spanish version of "Snow White," where the evil queen doesn't ask for the huntsman to bring back the heart of the princess—she asks him to fill a vial with Snow White's blood, stoppered with one of her severed toes.

Then I think of the story of Little Red Cap. Seems safe, seems happy. And I start the way every story starts, *"Once upon a time, there was a little girl . . ."* Grandpa stirs a little in his sleep, his arm lifting like he's greeting someone. I take this as a good sign and go on.

"Her name, stupidly enough, was Little Red Cap. Little Red Cap is supposed to bring some wine and bread to her sick grandmother, because those old Germans thought that some good booze would cure everything. And maybe they were right. I can ask Mom to sneak you some booze if you want some.

"Anyway, back to Little Red Cap. Her mom tells her not to talk to anyone on the road, to go straight to Grandma's. No detours. But of course she doesn't listen. Little Red Cap probably isn't that little. I bet she's a teenager, thinking her mom is all stupid and overprotective and scared of the forest. Maybe she thinks she's totally too old to be told what to do. Maybe she sits down by a tree and takes some hits off the wine, so when the wolf starts talking to her, she doesn't think, *My, what big teeth you have,* she thinks, *Hey, pooch, you're not so scary.* The wolf gets Grandma's address out of Little Red Cap, who's too drunk to notice, runs ahead along the road, gobbles Grandma, and waits for Little Red Cap to come stumbling along so he can eat her, too. And he does. She's just lucky that the huntsman's walking by when he is, that he hears that wolf snoring after such a big dinner. He cuts Little Red Cap and Grandma out of the wolf's belly, and everyone lives happily ever after."

Grandpa twitches in his sleep. I lean in closer, to whisper in his ear.

"But Grandpa, what if that's not what happened at all? What if Little Red Cap never veered off the road? What if she never even met the wolf or she got away from him? What if the huntsman just made all this stuff up and everybody believed him? What if he ruined Little Red Cap's reputation for all eternity? Just because he could?"

Grandma Emmy comes back to the room and brings us all back down to the cafeteria for dinner. We grab whatever looks edible—pizza and pasta and salad—and drag it to a table. Nobody's hungry but me. Mr. Doctor checks the messages with his answering service. Madge fiddles with her iPod, which is loaded with the most oppressive classical music she can find. June once burned a bunch of screamo for her, thinking it'd be right up Madge's alley, but Madge said, "What do I need this for? If I want to hear someone shrieking at me, I can just piss off Mom."

But Mom is quiet. She's been pretty quiet for almost thirty-six hours, which is beginning to sound an alarm in my head. Mom hasn't been so quiet for so long since Dad left, and who wants to go through that again?

I've eaten all the food except for one piece of pizza, and that's only because it has black olives on it, and I hate those. Madge turns off the iPod and pulls out the earbuds. Her face is shifting, her eyes growing bigger and darker and fangs creeping over her bottom lip, the jaw jutting like she's preparing to bite. For safety, I slide closer to the wall.

"Why didn't you say anything?" Madge says suddenly, in a low, ominous voice that promises pain, pain, and more pain. I tug on her sleeve, but she yanks her arm away.

"Say anything about what?" my mom says. She doesn't look at Madge but rummages around in her purse.

"That *isn't* bronchitis, Mom. I've had bronchitis, I know what bronchitis looks like, and that is not it!"

"It's a touch of pneumonia. I know he looks bad, but . . ." she says lamely, and trails off. This is so unlike her, the lameness, the trailing off. I want to bring up Mr. Mymer, distract her, energize her. I want to hand her the phone and tell her to call the school-board president, the principal, the police. I want to tell her what I did. That it's my fault. That there is an emergency and only she can save us.

"He has cancer, doesn't he?" says Madge.

"No," my mom says. "He doesn't have cancer." Her purse thumps to the floor. She doesn't pick it up. People at the surrounding tables are staring, but in the way people stare when they've been there themselves.

"Then something else," says Madge. "Some sort of emphysema or blood disease."

"No, he doesn't."

"What aren't you telling us?" Madge screams. Someone drops a tray, and the room is filled with the sounds of shattering glass. "We have a right to know what's happening!"

"I'm not keeping anything from you," Mom says. "I know this is hard, but what's happening is that your grandfather is an old man who caught a bad cold. The fluid settled in his lungs. Sometimes old people have a hard time with colds. Their hearts and their lungs don't work as well. They don't recover as quickly."

"Have you gone crazy?" Madge says. "This can't be from a cold."

"In the future," Mom says, "we'll have to be more careful when we go over for dinner. Make sure none of us has anything he could catch."

"In the future? What future? What are you talking about? Grandpa looks like he's going to die, and you're just sitting there talking about dinner. What is *wrong* with you?"

"Tiffany. I'm so sorry," my mom says. "This is just one of those things. It's going to take some time." She throws her hands up, once, twice. We're playing charades, guess which movie she's in now, the one with the crazy daughters, the one with the sick dad. "Grandpa loves you."

"That's not the point!"

"I love you."

"You don't love me," Madge says, biting the end off each word. "Nobody loves me."

My mom shakes her head and stares at the salad bar, blinking. It makes Madge insane. She doesn't need screamo; she *is* screamo. She starts shrieking at Mom, why didn't she tell us things were so bad, why does she keep saying that Grandpa will be fine, why is she so horrible, why is she so uncaring and stupid, why does she think *we're* stupid, Tola might be uncaring and stupid, but she, Madge, is not, and she is nineteen years old or almost and needs to understand exactly what's happening with her family, and if her own mother won't tell her, how is she supposed to live, that's what she wants to know, how am I supposed to live, Mom, how? How how how how how how how how how, until Mr. Doctor, who never says anything, who never gets involved, who drives everywhere without complaining, says in the calmest voice, "Tiffany. That's enough."

Madge is so shocked, she doesn't know what to do. She stares at Mr. Doctor as if she's never seen him before, as if he just sprang fully formed from the thin, cheap carpeting.

This time, she doesn't scream. She whispers. Somehow, it's louder. "I hate you."

Mr. Doctor nods. "I know. But does it matter right now?"

We go back to the room. Grandma Emmy naps in the big chair. Mom and Madge whisper-yell in the corner. Mr. Doctor leans against the wall.

I don't talk. I don't tell any stories. I hold Grandpa's hand. I squeeze. I think he squeezes back.

It's amazing to me. How holding someone's hand, something so small, could be so big.

(*comments*)

"As annoying as it is, there's a benefit to having a sister who doesn't remember much about her childhood. She doesn't remember any of the bad stuff you did to her, either. She doesn't remember the times you pinched her until she screamed. That you stole a drawing she made for your daddy and claimed it was your own. That there were two bath toys, a mermaid and a fish, and you always made her play with the fish. That you thought your parents loved her more, and sometimes you wished she had never been born."

—*Tiffany Riley, sister*

"One time, me and Spit found this website dedicated to this dead kid. I think he was sixteen. Get this: He tripped over his own shoelaces, hit his head on a curb, and died. I'm not kidding. So all his friends made this site and talked about him and how much he loved his iPod and that he was listening to his tunes when he died. We read this crap and couldn't stop laughing. We took some of the pictures of the kid from the website and pasted the kid's head on some porn. Spit found the kid's number and we cranked it. We'd say, 'Hey, Mom! I can tie my shoes!' Or 'I can't rest until you bury my iPod in my grave!'

"I passed Tola in the hallway, and she didn't even look at me. Someone told me that her grandpa was sick. Poor baby. Maybe I'll add something about that to the site. With a few skulls and crossbones, maybe pictures of graveyards. I could post the grandparents' phone number, so anyone looking for laughs can give a call."

—*Chelsea Patrick, classmate*

GEEK FORCE

Snow turns to rain turns to ice. The world is encased in glittering glass like Snow White was, beautiful and dead.

Thankfully, no more bio for me. I have a study in the library instead. Ms. Esme, the librarian, is in charge of my "studies." When she sees me, she grins and gives me a book on Joseph McCarthy.

I go to cooking class. The whole room smells like roasting chicken and onions. We figure the Duck is cooking a feast for the teachers' holiday party. Just to taunt us.

She passes out the recipes for the mayonnaise again. Plain, spicy, mango-chutney. Drop, drop, drop. We are old pros. We finish in a few minutes: no accidents with the eggs or the oil.

The Duck passes out a second set of recipes. Not for more mayo, but for sandwiches. Chicken with peppers and spicy mayonnaise in a tortilla. Chicken with red peppers and mango-chutney mayo on wheat. Chicken with lettuce, bacon, and tomato and plain mayo on rye. For the vegetarians, she has a recipe for a roasted vegetable sandwich with sundried-tomato mayo.

The Duck takes the chicken and the vegetables out of the oven. Nobody asks the question, but she answers it anyway.

"It's cold outside," says the Duck. "I thought we could all use some comfort food."

Mr. Mymer isn't back yet, so we have another sub in art. She is round and happy, with a gray halo of hair and earrings made from red Christmas ornaments. She shows us pictures of her cats. They are all named after hobbits. Bilbo, Merry, Pippin, Rosie, Myrtle. She tells us to pick a cat and draw, paint, or sculpt it. I draw my own cat. I give him a hat, a sword, and a sweet pair of boots.

After school, Mr. Doctor picks me up, drives me home. Madge is watching one of her movies. I've brought home the drawing of Pib, which I think I can turn into a painting.

I set up in my room. First, I do some studies—sketching what the painting might look like. Then I get out my paints and palette and start mixing some colors for the fur—white and sienna and bronze. It smells good. It feels good. It's been a good day. Grandpa's still sick, but Mom's visiting him alone tonight and hopes to pin the doctors down on the treatment. Madge is still crazy, but she's taking some medicine and maybe it will work. Mr. Mymer is coming back. Maybe I'm coming back, too.

Madge kicks open my door. She sits on my bed and opens her laptop. Pib tries to walk across the keyboard, but she shoves him off. She brings up The Truth About Tola Riley on screen. Chelsea's saved the best for last: ART, A STATUTORY LOVE STORY. It's a grainy video of me and Mr. Mymer at the museum, slowed down and jazzed up. You see the talking, the smiling, the paging through the Klimt book, me reaching for his hand, holding it. My face, so naked, so hungry, so obvious. The images morph and blend, changing colors like Andy Warhol prints. Scrolling underneath the video is a series of quotes and comments: *this girl is a crazy skank, i heard she totally did Michael Brandeis too, he's sooooo ugly! eewwwww,* and on and on.

And over it all is the sound of my voice, from the day Chelsea Patrick turned me into a happy face: "Sorry for what? Sorry for what? Sorry for what?"

When Mr. Doctor gets home, I ask him to drive me to the mall. I find her at the electronics store where she works. I crouch in the video game section across the aisle, watching. She's in the computer department, stocking the shelves with adapters and flash drives while a bunch of guys wearing Geek Force T-shirts hang around the shiny new Macs, not doing much of anything. A girl walks by, one of those stick figures with boobs, and the guys stare and nudge one another.

"Can I help you, miss?" one of them says.

The girl barely glances at him. "I don't think so."

Another says, "How about your number?"

She rolls her eyes and keeps walking. The guys' smiles get tight and fake. I don't know what they expected, or maybe she did exactly what stick figures with boobs always did to them. Either way, they're mad and looking for someone to take it out on. Their eyes find *her*, carefully hanging plastic packages on hooks. They glance around, probably making sure there's no manager around to stop them.

Then: "Hey, Patrick. Wanna go out sometime?"

She doesn't answer, but even from where I'm hiding I can see the blood that burns in her cheeks.

"You're sooo hot," says the one who asked for the stick girl's number. "Do you do three-ways?"

Chelsea lifts up her head and glares, which only makes them snicker. And I guess here's where I'm supposed to feel sorry for her, where I discover that she's in pain, too, mocked by a bunch of angry, overcompensating woman-haters with hairballs for brains. And maybe I *would* have felt sorry for her if she didn't drop the basket of adapters and stomp over to the Geek Force, dispersing them like bunny rabbits. If she didn't see me crouched on the floor across the aisle, pretending to study the latest version of Grand Theft Auto.

Her eyes narrow, then she smirks. "Looking for something? We've got *lots* of computers with *tons* of memory. Great for watching videos on the internet."

I shove the game back on the shelf and stand to face her. "My computer's fine. It's the psycho in my school who's giving me all the problems."

She breaks out in a grin. "Did you know there was an exhibit about digital art that day you and Mr. Mymer went to the museum? That's what I was there to see. Lots of good stuff, but none of it went far enough, in my opinion. Sort of dead on arrival. Bland electronic imitations of two-dimensional art. I filmed them anyway; I've got a great camera and I know how to hide it from the guards. But none of it had the right impact. And then, there you were with Mymer. God. The look on your face! Pure desperation."

"What is wrong with you?"

"You told the school board nothing was going on," she says, thoroughly enjoying herself. "Why would you care what I put online? I mean, if nothing was happening."

"Nothing *was* happening."

"Sure. Whatever you say. I can't help what *other people* will say about it, though."

My whole body is buzzing, I'm so angry. I suddenly understand every bit of violence in every fairy tale I've ever read. The ovens, the axes, the cauldrons full of snakes and lizards and the urge to shove people into them. People always say there are two sides to every story, but I don't believe that's true. Not always. There are villains in this world who do terrible things. *Why* they do them is something else.

"Why?" I say.

"Because you're a stupid slut."

"Cut the crap."

"Being a slut isn't enough?"

In stories, the villains launch into their confessions, spilling their guts as soon as you ask the right question: *I want to be the most beautiful in the land. I want to marry the prince. I want the throne for myself. I'll get you, my pretty, and your little dog, too.*

"We were friends for a long time," I say.

"So we played hopscotch in the third grade. I'm supposed to feel bad?"

"You're supposed to feel *something*."

"You think you can do anything," she says.

"Climb every mountain? Swim every sea?"

"Paint your stupid paintings—God, those paintings! They're like pages from a bad calendar you get at the dollar store. And Mymer! You never shut up about him. Mr. Mymer *loves* my work. Mr. Mymer thinks I'm sooo talented."

Did I say that? Did I lie? "He never even complimented me." And now that I'm saying it, I realize it's true. He talked to me, he encouraged me, he pushed me, but he never told me I was a great painter. Not once.

"All because you screwed him," Chelsea's saying.

"You screwed yourself," I say. "There are actually laws against stalking."

"Whatever. No one will be able to trace the site or the video or anything back to me, and every time your mother gets it shut down, I can get it back up somewhere else. To the police, I'm just a concerned student worried that my old friend is being abused, that's all."

"If you had that video the whole time, why did you wait until now to post it?" But even as I'm saying it, I know why. Because waiting until now just prolongs the fun for her, and the agony for me.

"You're sick," I say. "Something happened to you. What happened to you?"

"I told everyone that I'll put the best comments in the piece. There are already hundreds of new ones," she says, smiling evilly. "Everyone wants to be a part of my little video. I love reading them. It's like the world's best bedtime story. Puts me right to sleep."

"Someone should do that permanently."

She takes two giant steps forward and puts her face in mine. "Are you going to do it?" She pokes me in the chest. "With what? The power of your thoughts?"

She pokes me again. I grab her finger. She tries to pull away, but I'm locked down. She yanks harder, dragging me into the aisle with her. I don't care. I've been punched by the best of them.

"Don't you get it? You can't win," she says. Her breath smells bad, like something inside her died long ago. "You're useless. What are you going to do, paint a picture?"

"What's going on here?"

Our heads whip around to see a guy way too young for the enormous gut straining his Geek Force T-shirt. The white tag on his chest says CHUCK HUGHES: ASSISTANT MANAGER.

"I asked you a question. What's going on?"

I let go of Chelsea's finger. She takes a step back.

Both of us, in unison: "Nothing."

"Looked like something to me. Chelsea? You want to explain?"

"We were just talking, Mr. Hughes," she says.

He looks from her to me, raising his shaggy unibrow. I could do some damage here, I know, tell this guy that she wanted to beat me up, tell him that she wanted to sell me stolen televisions. But it won't be the right kind of damage. And it won't be enough.

"It's like she says. We were just catching up. We know each other from school."

"From school, huh?" He frowns. "You seem familiar to me. Don't I know you?"

"No," I say, turning to go. "People just think they do."

Afterward, I have to wait in front of the corner department store for Mr. Doctor. He pulls up in his hybrid SUV.

"Thanks for picking me up," I say.

He grunts cheerfully in reply. He puts the car in gear and drives. As I sink into my seat, I realize how much I love this car, the murmur of the engine, the whir of the fan, the radio. It saves me from attempting the smallest small talk, not that Mr. Doctor needs it. In Mr. Doctor's car, you're safe, even if it's only for the time it takes to get where you're going.

I ask Mr. Doctor to turn up the heat, and he does. All around us, the town glistens. Icicles hang from telephone lines, ice coats the trees. I wonder how the trees survive, weighed down like that. I wonder how they don't break.

Mr. Doctor turns up the radio. His favorite talk radio show yammers on about the removal of a judge who threw forty-six people in jail after no one would admit to owning the cell phone that rang in his court. A Japanese man was arrested for releasing hundreds of beetle larvae inside an express train to try to scare female passengers.

And then this:

"In local news, a teacher recently exonerated by police and reinstated to his teaching position is again under suspicion over a video released anonymously on the internet. The teacher, Al Mymer, was investigated for an alleged affair with a student, but police found no evidence of the affair. Last night, however, a video showing the teacher and the same student holding hands at a New York City museum café popped up on a website, casting doubt on the result of the police investigation.

"In response to this new evidence, Al Mymer released this statement:

"'It is with great sadness that I resign my position at

Willow Park High School. I was thrilled to be exonerated of all charges of wrongdoing and planned to return to my job, but it is clear to me today nothing will change the fact that my reputation, and the reputation of my student, have been permanently damaged. I sincerely hope she can get on with her life. And I will have to move on with mine. I thank everyone on the staff of Willow Park High School and the parents and students who wrote letters supporting me. I will miss you all.'"

My eyes water, but it isn't the heat blasting from the vents. It's my voice blasting from my throat.

"It's my fault," I say. "It's all my fault. I was at the museum café. I was sitting alone. He just happened to be there at the same time, and he sat with me. He was always so nice. And I was . . . lonely."

I stare straight ahead. I don't know who I'm telling. The windshield. The ice-encased trees. The road.

"I touched him. Just his hand, and just the once, but it was me, not him. And only for a few seconds before he pulled away. He never told anybody what I did, but then I never told anybody what I did, either. At first, I didn't say anything because I was embarrassed. And then later, I didn't say anything because it all seemed so stupid." I want to cry. I *should* cry, big ugly Madge-sized sobs. But I'm all locked up inside.

Mr. Doctor says what he always says: nothing.

Then Mr. Doctor opens his mouth. "I love to drive."

I turn to stare at him.

"People think I'm crazy, but I love it."

I sit perfectly still, wondering what the hell is going on.

"When I was young," he says, "I used to drive and drive and drive, hoping that I would get lost."

I'm still staring at him, but he keeps his eyes on the road. Mr. Safety, Mr. Doctor is, even now.

"But I never got lost," he says, his voice heavy with disappointment. "I seem to have a compass in my head."

He doesn't speak for ten more minutes. Not till we're turning onto our block.

"I could teach you, if you want."

(comments)

"At first, I did stuff the way the other trolls did. Just for laughs. We call them lulz. You'd be amazed how many people you can freak out just by calling them on their bullshit. It was delicious. But sometimes I get tired of people not knowing who I am. Sometimes I want credit. That thing with the superintendent showed me that.

"It's not trolling. It's art."

—*Chelsea Patrick, classmate*

"My first wife always wanted kids. But I said we had to wait. I was still in dental school. We had no time. We had no money. We lived in a studio apartment.

"So we waited. And then, right after I graduated, she was killed in a car accident. I think of her when I see Anita's girls. They're a handful, I guess, but I think that she would have liked them."

—*Dr. Anthony Baldini, stepfather*

THE BATH

Grandpa Joe is sitting up and seems focused on what I'm saying, which I hope is a good sign. He's dropped ten pounds he can't afford to lose since he's been in the hospital, but he manages a couple of bites of the cupcake that I brought for him. It's a cupcake I found in my locker and saved especially for Grandpa. The doctors say every bite counts, and these cupcakes have an obscene pillow of buttercream frosting.

"More cupcake, Grandpa?"

"I think I've had enough for now."

"Come on. When have you ever refused dessert in your whole life?"

"Maybe some water."

I swallow my disappointment and carefully wrap the cupcake in a napkin in case he wants another bite later. Then I take the cup of water and hold the straw so he can take a sip. I wipe the drips from his chin with the sleeve of my favorite tattered sweater.

"Thank you," he says. "What day is it? How long have I been here?"

"I don't know exactly," I tell him. "A couple of weeks?"

"I feel like it's been a month. Or a year."

"I feel like that, too, Grandpa."

"Where's Grandma?"

"Getting soda from the machine in the cafeteria with Mom and Madge."

"Oh," he says, and suddenly closes his eyes. Each time he does this, my heart starts to pound. Sometimes I run out into the hallway where they have the monitors for the whole floor mounted on the wall so that the nurses can keep an eye on the patients' vitals. I watch to make sure that *his* heart is still beating, that the waves dart up and down the way they should, as if I actually know what that would look like.

His eyes flash open, and he tries to sit up higher in the bed. I've watched the nurses help him a million times, so I do what they do: I grab the sides of the quilted pad laid beneath him and use that to haul him up rather than tugging at his arms and at the delicate skin that hangs like swaths of wrinkled cotton from his bones. It's harder than it looks.

"You're getting good at that," he says. I have to lean in close to hear him. "Wouldn't think you'd be so strong."

"I'm *your* granddaughter."

"True," he says. "So what's going on with that teacher of yours?"

"Oh, nothing. He quit. He found another job, I think." As I say this, my voice cracks. But Grandpa doesn't notice. He's closed his eyes again.

"How's everyone doing?" my mom says from the doorway. Her voice sounds like she's forcing it through clenched teeth.

"Okay," Grandpa breathes. Grandma Emmy comes in and holds his hand. Madge paces in the background.

"He ate some of the cupcake I brought," I say.

"Yeah, now he's cured," Madge mutters.

Mom ignores Madge. "That's great, Dad."

"I think I might have an emergency," he says, trying to throw the sheet off.

"Let me get a nurse," Mom says.

"I need to use the bathroom," Grandpa says.

"It's no problem," says Mom. "Let me help you."

"I don't need help," he says.

"Yes, Dad, you do. You're not strong enough to walk on your own." She suddenly notices me and Madge. "Give us some privacy, girls."

Madge grabs me by the elbow and drags me from the room. When we're out in the hallway, she says, "Nice going."

"What do you mean?"

"The cupcake?"

"He has to eat," I say.

"It goes right through him."

I'm sick of Grandpa being sick. And I'm sick of Madge being Madge. I'm so sick of her that the sickness is a living thing, a spiked briar that twists up from my stomach and twines itself around my throat. "So we shouldn't try? We should be like you and just give up?"

"What do you mean?"

"Never mind."

"I want to know what you mean."

"No, you don't," I say. "You don't want to know what anyone means. You just want to stay as miserable as possible. We should go outside and dig a hole so that you can jump in and get it over with."

She glowers at me like a thunderhead. But I glower back—harder, fiercer—and for once she's the one who drops her head first.

On the way home, the silence is truly glacial, a frozen crust even the hum of the engine and the yammering of the radio can't cut through. The doctors are now giving Grandpa something to make food more palatable, and something to help him hold on to it, but if a cupcake isn't palatable, I don't know what is.

Mom drops Grandma off at her house. "Mom, are you sure you don't want to come home with us?"

"I'm fine, Annie," Grandma says. She's the only one in

the universe who calls my mom Annie instead of Anita. Not even Grandpa can get away with it. Must be something about mothers. Mothers can get away with stuff presidents can't.

"I want to be in my own house," Grandma says.

"I can make dinner for you."

"No, no, no. I'm not hungry," Grandma says. "I'll call you tomorrow."

"Mom—"

Grandma pats her roughly on the arm and scoots out of the car before Mom can say anything else. We watch Grandma march up the sidewalk to her door, her purse clutched under her arm like a football. If I know her, she'll make herself a peanut butter and jelly sandwich and eat it with a pickle. Or she'll forget to eat completely.

Mom sighs and puts the car in gear. She's erratic on the road, slipping over the line here, drifting there, but we don't mention it. We also don't mention the fact that she scrapes the side of the garage with the car on the way in.

"How about breakfast for dinner?" she says once we're inside the house.

I shrug. Madge shrugs.

"Well," Mom says. "*I* want breakfast for dinner, so that's what I'm making. Pancakes, eggs, and bacon."

"Shouldn't we have some sort of vegetable?" says Madge.

"I'll slice you a tomato."

"That's a fruit," Madge says.

Mom doesn't answer. She goes into the kitchen and gets

out the griddle and a couple of frying pans. It takes only about fifteen minutes for her to fill a few platters with food and get them on the table. When we were little, this was our favorite meal of all time—Mom's, too—because it was so easy. But now it seems weird to enjoy it when Grandpa can't, and when Grandma is alone in her house playing solitaire.

I'm trying to find the right way to tell my mom about Mr. Mymer, if she doesn't already know from her husband. But Madge jumps in first.

"Where's the ever-important orthodontist?" says Madge, pushing some eggs around her plate. Pib perches in Mr. Doctor's seat, praying for bacon.

Mom takes pity on Pib, shredding a few bits of bacon and putting them on the table in front of him. "He had some late appointments," Mom says. "He'll be back later."

"He couldn't cancel them to go with us to the hospital?" Madge says. "What kind of husband is he?"

Mom pushes her plate to the center of the table, stands, and walks out of the room. Upstairs, we hear the bathroom door close and then the water pouring into the tub.

I stand up, too, and start clearing the plates.

"I'm not done," Madge says.

I take her plate. "Yeah, you are."

Most of the food gets dumped into the garbage, and the plates and platters loaded into the dishwasher. By the time I'm through, I'm the only one left in the kitchen; even Pib has found some new haunt. The water is still running. I examine my fingernails, which are stained with paint and ink. I should take a bath when Mom is finished. Wash it all away.

In the family room, I flip on the TV and try to find something to kill time. Reality show, reality show, reality show. Singing, dancing, dog grooming. I pick dog grooming. A vicious white poodle terrorizes a groomer with a pink mullet. Pink Mullet Woman doesn't have a chance. She's booted from the competition after she's bitten repeatedly, and the dog is criticized for the uneven puffball that is now his head. In her parting interview, Mullet Woman cries, her face going as pink as her hair. She looks stupid. I decide that it might be a good time to dye my hair back to its original brown. Plus, her mullet reminds me of Chelsea Patrick, and I want a bath more than ever.

I go upstairs to check if Mom will be out of the tub sometime this century. I find Madge sitting in the hallway next to the bathroom door, Pib stretched across her knees.

"What are you doing?"

"Shhh!" she says.

"What?"

"Mom's crying."

"I thought she was taking a bath."

She rolls her eyes. "She turned the water on so we couldn't hear her."

"And I guess you're here to remind her that water is a precious natural resource that shouldn't be wasted?"

I expect her to glower at me again, but, like Mom, Madge

isn't always so predictable. Her lips curl up in a ghost of a smile and she scratches Pib behind the ears. "Getting sassy in your old age, aren't you?"

"That's my cat."

"And?"

"He hates you."

"Funny way of showing it."

I slide down the wall and sit next to her. Behind the crash of the water, I hear the faint sounds of weeping. I haven't heard my mother cry in a long time, not since we watched a special on Animal Planet about the melting ice caps and the plight of polar bears.

"I don't like it when she cries," Madge says.

"Me neither."

"What should we do about it?"

"You're asking me?"

"No, I'm asking the bloody cat."

"I don't know what to do," I say. "I don't know what to do about anything." I bang the back of my head against the wall. "You know what I did? I actually went to see Chelsea Patrick. Confront her. Like that was going to serve an actual purpose. She's twice my size. She could eat me for a snack."

"Wait," she says. "Chelsea Patrick? The one you were friends with in middle school?"

"She's the one who spread the rumors. She's the police's 'witness.' She's the one who put up the stupid video. What was I supposed to do? Let her get away with it?"

213

"You knew who posted that thing? Why didn't you say so?"

"I thought you knew," I say. "And, besides, you never asked."

"You mean I wasn't interested."

"That, too."

"Well," she says. "It's not surprising."

"That you weren't interested?"

"That Chelsea put up the video."

"Why do you say that?"

"Oh, I don't know. Because she's a sociopath, maybe? She freaked me out whenever she came here. Always talking about her creepy online friends. I didn't know what you saw in her. I thought she was a freak."

"If she wasn't then, she is now."

"And isn't her mom that nutball who's trying to get the books banned?"

"That's her. She was at the school-board meeting when they talked about Mr. Mymer. I think she got cheek implants or something. She sort of looks like one of those decorative masks they put up at Chinese restaurants."

"Nice."

We're quiet for a minute. The faucet is still running full blast. Pretty soon Mom will have depleted the stores of potable water for the entire tri-state area.

"Do you think she's going to be in there for a long time? I have something I want to tell her."

"I don't think she's in the mood to talk right now," Madge says.

"Mr. Mymer resigned 'cause of that video. I heard it on the news. I'm surprised Mom hasn't said anything yet."

"I think she's more worried about Grandpa."

"I know. But that video proves I didn't tell the truth. At least, I didn't tell the whole truth. We bumped into each other at the museum and he sat with me for a while. I always had a little crush on him—"

"Oh, Tola," she says, covering her face.

"And he was sitting so close to me. I grabbed his hand. I just wanted to hold it."

"What did he do?"

That part wasn't on the video. "He pulled away. And then he got up and left. I think he was disappointed in me."

"And that's it?"

"That's it," I say.

"Why didn't you just tell Mom what happened in the first place? Don't you think it would have been easier?"

"I was embarrassed about it. I was so stupid. And then I was angry that she didn't believe me when I said he didn't hurt me. This is all my fault."

"Oh, it is not. So you touched the guy's hand. So what? You didn't rip off your clothes and run naked around the museum."

"I still can't understand why she didn't believe me. It's like she's been mad at me for so long. Mad at you, too. Everyone's so mad all the time."

"Yeah, well. That could be my fault."

"What are you talking about?"

"As long as we're confessing and everything . . . remember the affidavit I wrote for Dad?"

"Yeah. What about it?"

"I wrote about us being able to visit who we wanted when we wanted, just like I told you. But I also wrote about Mom kissing Mr. Rosentople. And I said that you saw it, too."

"You did *what*?"

"I said that she was probably having an affair and that should be taken into account when the custody arrangements were made. I blamed the divorce on her. I thought if she didn't harass Dad all the time about his work, he wouldn't have left. Ever since he hooked up with the Saxon She-Beast, he never calls and we never get to see him. I was pissed off."

"Did Mom see this affa-thing?"

"Sure. It's a court document."

"What did she say?"

"She said that Mr. Rosentople kissed her and not the other way around. And it only happened once. And that Dad was already emotionally 'gone' from the marriage."

"But you don't believe it."

She hesitates. "Dad was, you know, like me. Not really into other people's problems, thinking about himself a lot. I knew Mom was lonely. Sometimes when Mr. Rosentople came over, she would flirt with him." Madge shudders, and Pib shifts in her lap, gnawing on one of her fingers. "But now? My therapist says that maybe she wanted a little attention and that's as far as it went. That Mom didn't have anything to do with it."

"Huh. What else does your therapist say?"

Madge gives me a look. "What are you implying?"

"I think this therapist is getting to you."

"Maybe." She pets Pib, long strokes from head to tail. "You know, I remember everything that happens to me. Since I was two."

"Don't rub it in."

"It's not a gift. It's a curse. I've spent a lot of time trying to figure out why I feel so crappy all the time, combing through my memories. Like, there must have been some point where I went wrong."

"You're kidding," I say. "I've been thinking the same thing because I *can't* remember anything."

"Well, it doesn't help. You read books about girls who are depressed, and a lot of times there's a certain reason. They were robbed or raped or their fathers beat them or something. So, our parents got divorced. But plenty of people's parents get divorced and their kids don't cry all the time. They don't feel like they're drowning. And then I realized that it wasn't any one thing. It was me. It was *in* me. In my head. What do you do about that?"

"I don't know," I say. I remember—I'm sure this is my

own memory, that this doesn't come from some book or movie or whatever—taking baths with my sister when we were very, very small. I remember a yellow plastic fish with a spout in it, a mermaid doll with pink hair. (Tiffany always made me play with the fish.) And that one day, Tiffany-who-was-not-yet-Madge informed me that her imaginary friend Po Po would be joining us to play, and that Po Po would need to borrow the fish. I told Mom that I wanted to take my own baths alone, and my mom said it was time for that anyway.

I wonder if this means that we left Madge before she left us. I put my hand on her knee.

"I asked this stupid therapist that question. What do you do if the problem's in your head? What if you can't find the exact moment everything turned to shit? And he said forget the past. You start from today. From right now. You say, fine, I'm depressed. And it sucks. So how am I going to help myself?"

"How do you?"

She sighs, a sigh so hard that it seems to come from the bottom of her lungs. "I do my therapist's bloody homework. I keep journals. I started . . ." She swallows hard. "I started taking medication."

"I know," I say. "I saw the bottle."

"It scares me. It might be dangerous. It might not work. But staying the way I was scares me more. Anyway, I'm lucky I'm *able* to do something about it. Some people can't even get out of bed."

I realize that my mom has turned the water off. Pib meows suddenly, piteously, until Madge rubs his belly.

"Remember when we were little kids, and Mom was always yelling at us to get out of the bathtub?" Madge says.

"I remember that you stole my plastic fish. I think that's the only memory I have of my entire childhood."

"I think it's time to get over the fish," she says. "But do you remember the way we used to call Mom when we wanted to get out of the tub?"

"Uh . . ."

"God, you are totally hopeless, aren't you? Can you remember your own name?"

"Sister of Satan?"

"We used to call Mom by saying 'Mommy' really, really soft. And then again a little louder. Then louder, and louder, and louder until we were screaming."

"If you say so."

"We should do that now."

"What?"

"Scream 'Mommy, Mommy, Mommy.'"

"Why?"

"I don't know. I just think we should do it."

"I'm not doing that," I say.

"Why not?"

"'Cause it's stupid."

"You weren't too proud before."

"What was I? Three years old?"

"So?"

"And people think I'm weird," I say.

"Everyone's weird," says Madge.

"If everyone's weird, then no one is."

Madge grins, actually grins, suddenly, mysteriously delighted. "Finally, she's catching on."

"Madge."

"What?"

"You're smiling."

"And?"

"Well, it's not something you do very often."

"I'm on drugs," she says bluntly.

"But . . ." I say. "It hasn't been long enough. What if it's just that placebo effect? What if it's not real?"

"As long as it works, it's real," she says. "Come on, let's do the Mommy thing. She'll like it."

Madge unceremoniously shoves a surprised Pib off her lap and crawls to the bathroom. I can't leave her to make a fool of herself, and I want to keep her happy as long as possible, so I follow. We crouch by the door. She holds up fingers: one, two, three. And together, softly, as soft as we can, we whisper:

"Mommy."

We wait another few seconds, and do it again, just the slightest bit louder: "Mommy."

And louder: "Mommy."

Louder: "Mommy."

And then suddenly something in my moth-eaten memory clicks. I can feel my wrinkled fingertips, the suck of moisture in my chest, and the cooling water on my skin. I can smell the coconut and pineapple of the store-brand bubble bath. I can hear us both, our little voices, starting quietly and then building. I must be smiling, too, because Madge's grin blazes back. I let myself remember that I once had a mom and a dad, a big sister and a plastic fish, a sunny grandma and a grandpa who would push me on the swings and tell me that one day I would be a great artist. That there was a time before the divorce and sickness and the misunderstandings, a time where nobody told me I was weird and maybe didn't even believe I was, or if they believed it, they didn't care. And I'm still screaming—mommymommymommy—but it's different now. I'm laughing and crying at the same time, because the remembering is so good but so sad.

The bathroom door flies open and she stands over us, so tall, tall as that mom from a long time ago. She bends and gathers us both in her arms like we're three years old and six years old, quaking with the cold and the damp and the sudden realization that we're all alone in the world.

(*comments*)

"What she did seemed innocent to me. Misguided but sweet. I made it clear that it was unacceptable, made a mental note to confer with the school psychologist in the beginning of the next week. Other students have done similar things over the years, crossed the line a bit, so I never thought to make her action public. It never occurred to me that things would get so out of hand. I didn't understand the depth of some people's hysteria. I can't believe some of the articles and blog postings being written about this. Obscene. It's almost as if they wanted it to be true.

"People ask me who is to blame for what happened. I want to say: you. All of *you*."

—*Albert Mymer, art teacher*

GLASS SLIPPER

It takes me a couple of days, but I tell my mom the whole story. That I touched Mr. Mymer, but he didn't do anything to me. I tell her that Chelsea was the one spreading the rumors. That she posted the video. That she was probably the one who started the Truth About Tola Riley blog, though I didn't have actual proof of any of it.

She wants to call the cops. She wants to call the counselors. She wants to call the president. I tell her she should worry about Grandpa. That I'm okay. And that when Grandpa was okay, too, we could go back to the school board. I would tell them the truth. I would tell everyone.

She's too tired and too worried about Grandpa to argue. And, anyway, I'm lying again.

I call June. "Hello?" She sounds cautious and hesitant. "It's me. Tola."

"Did you call me?"

"Of course I called you. Your phone rang, didn't it?"

"It keeps calling other people."

"That's because it's alive," I say.

"It's been calling Pete Santorini and Alex Nobody-Can-Pronounce-His-Last-Name."

"Ew."

"They're not so bad."

"They're not?"

"No, they can be nice. They send me photos. They have decent bodies."

I figure her phone must have shoved some sort of electronic tentacle into her brain and vacuumed out an important lobe. The sanity lobe. The dignity lobe. "Listen, June. You have to meet me at the school on Saturday night. Seven o'clock."

"Huh? Why?"

"Bring your dad's tools."

"You want me to break into the school?"

"We might not have to. There's a football game, and the doors could be open. If not, though, I'll need the tools. Besides, I need supplies and stuff and the janitors always lock the closets."

"Why do you need to get into the school?"

"Chelsea gave me an idea."

"Chelsea? What kind of idea?"

"She reminded me of 'The Goose Girl.' It's a Grimm's

story where this creepy girl tries to steal the throne by imper-
sonating a princess. But the king finds out. He asks the fake
princess how she'd punish a usurper. She says that she'd strip
the girl naked, put her in a barrel studded with nails, and
drag her through the streets until she's dead. And the king
says, 'Okay, that's what we're going to do to you.'"

"What a sweet story. I'll tell it to my children. What does
it have to do with Chelsea?"

"Let's just say that she's kind of like the fake princess. She
gave me the idea for her own punishment. So, are you in?"

"I can't, Tola. I have to volunteer at a soup kitchen on
Saturday night."

"Would it help if I told you that your phone wants you
to meet me?"

"My mother says—"

"It will look good on your college applications, I know,"
I say. "June, what are you going to study in college?"

"What do you mean? What everybody studies. Lit, math,
science, that kind of thing."

"And why are you taking all these AP classes and college
courses?"

"Why are you asking me these stupid questions, Tola?
You know why. So I can place out of—"

"All your college classes. So let me ask you again. What
classes are you taking in college? After AP Calculus, AP
History, AP English, AP Bio, AP Chemistry, AP Physics,
AP AP, the peacemakers seminar, the leadership seminar,

the seminar to learn how to take seminars, and 'Whiteness: The Other Side of Racism,' what's left?"

"Very funny. If I test out of all the basics, I can graduate early."

"And do what?"

"Whatever I want."

"Which is?"

There's silence. Then: "You're being an asshole."

"No, I'm making a point. How about doing something *you* want to do for a change, instead of something your mom thinks you should do?"

"And you honestly think I want to help you break into a school?"

"Of course you do. You'll be helping me to be a rebel while turning into a rebel yourself. Plus, when was the last time we did something together outside of lunch in the cafeteria?"

"I made out with you in the art room."

"What have you done for me *lately*?"

"Okay, okay," she says. "Fine. I'll meet you."

"And in case my mom calls, tell your phone that I'm sleeping at your house. We're going to a seminar."

"If you get me arrested," she says, "it's not going to look good on my applications."

School, hospital, school, hospital. I spend the next few days going back and forth between the two. Sometimes

Grandpa is better; sometimes he's the same. The doctors tell us to be patient, that the pneumonia is gone, he's off the antibiotics, and his body will return to normal. And then they remind us that Grandpa is a very old man and that "normal" is relative. Helpful, those doctors. My mother grills them so hard that they now run the other way when they see her coming.

It's Saturday afternoon. I tell my mom that June and I are going to the movies and then attending a Sunday seminar on college admissions. Mom's thrilled. She buys me a brand-new notebook and a pack of fancy pens so that I can take notes. She says she will kiss Grandpa for me.

The school parking lot is packed, and random groups of kids roam the grounds. The building lights are off, but someone has shoved a piece of cardboard between the side entrance door and the jamb. We slip inside without anyone noticing. June is disappointed, because she really wanted to try out her father's tools.

But she gets her chance when we get to Mr. Mymer's art room. The outer door isn't locked, but the door to the supply closet is.

"The first step," she says, "is to insert the tension wrench into the keyhole."

"Bored!"

"You're hopeless."

She kneels by the door, inserts the tension wrench—which looks more like a skinny screwdriver—and then another pick. She jiggles the picks around, listening for a click. She has to jiggle for fifteen minutes before the door opens.

"Remind me never to rob a bank with you," I say.

We creep into the dark closet and close the door behind us. We'll have to hide for a couple of hours, long enough to make sure that the school is empty. I brought a backpack with my paints, brushes, a camera, a deck of cards, and a flashlight.

"What? No snacks?" says June.

"Crap," I say.

Two hours and a nap later, we're pretty sure the coast is clear. We carefully open the door to the supply closet and sneak from the room. In the hallway, we listen for sounds of football players or cheerleaders, janitors or teachers. Nothing. It's horror-movie dark. It's horror-movie quiet.

"Boo," I whisper.

"Oh, shut up," June says.

We creep to the front of the school, to the long white hallway across from the principal's office. It's freshly primed, blank, and perfect.

While June randomly texts, I unpack the paints and brushes I brought. Like I thought, I'll need more paint. We go back to the supply closet and load up on big tubes of acrylics and some larger brushes. I grab an extra palette for mixing colors, some charcoal for sketching, and a roll of paper towels. We make one last trip for a short stepladder. And then I'm ready.

There's a banging noise. I jump. June grins.

"What's that?"

"Snacks," she says. She runs around the corner. I hear her unlock the front door. A familiar voice echoes in the hallway.

June comes back around the corner, Seven behind her. He's carrying a thermos and a tin box with snowflakes all over it. He opens it and shows me about a dozen expertly frosted cupcakes. All have the number 7 on them.

"Hey," I say. "Where did you get these?"

"I made them," he says.

"You made them? From a mix?"

"Are you kidding? Didn't I ever tell you? I want to be a pastry chef."

"Oh my God," I say. "You really are."

"I really am what?"

"You'll see."

While I sketch out what I want to do on the wall, June and Seven sprawl on the floor. They play cards and take turns holding the flashlight for me. We ask one another what's your favorite color; what's the most embarrassing song on your iPod; what would you do if you won a million dollars in the lottery; if you had to choose between riding an elevator for six months straight or being completely bald for five years, which would you pick?

After they fall asleep, I hold the flashlight for myself.

At about two in the morning, I take a coffee break. It's cold and it's gross, but I drink it anyway. Then I slip June's phone from her hand and creep down the hall so that I don't wake them up.

I know he's still awake. He never sleeps.

"Wha? Hello?"

Okay, now he sleeps.

"Hi, Dad."

"Tola? Is something wrong?"

"No, everything's okay."

Sheets rustle. "It's two in the morning."

"I know. I'm sorry. I thought you'd be awake."

"Is she crazy?" a woman's voice moans. *"It's two A.M."*

"Look, Dad. Sorry I woke you. I just wanted to let you know that the school needs to see you on Monday morning for a meeting."

"This couldn't wait until tomorrow?"

"No, it couldn't."

"Monday? What's this about?"

The woman: *"We're not available Monday."*

"That's pretty short notice, Tola. I just don't see how I can swing it. I've got work, and Hannalore is preparing to show a new artist at the gallery. I hope you understand."

I say, "Dad?"

"What, honey?"

"Hannalore can bite my apple."

There's a pause on the other end of the line. "I don't think that's called for."

"And so can you."

"Tola, I—"

"Bye, Dad. See you Monday, bright and early, seven thirty."

I paint all night.

When I get back home on Sunday afternoon, tired and wired, I find my mom at the door, jangling her car keys. "They're transferring your grandfather to a rehab center," she tells me. "We have to sign some paperwork, move him by ambulance, and get him settled into the new place."

"A rehab center? Does that mean he's getting better?"

"I hope so," she says, and hugs me. She's been hugging us a lot since that day we screamed in front of the bathroom door, hugging us so much that Madge bleats, *"Will you* please *get off me, Mother?"* even though you can tell she doesn't really mean it.

It's just me and Mom on either side of Grandpa Joe's bed. Madge and Grandma Emmy are at the nurses' station asking about Grandpa Joe's favorite sweater, which Grandma insisted she left in the closet and is now missing. Grandpa is dressed in sweatpants and a long-sleeved T-shirt. He looks about ten years older than he did just a month ago. But his eyes are open, and he's sitting up.

"When do I get out of here?" he says.

"When the nurse comes, Dad," my mom tells him.

"You said that a half hour ago."

"Mom has them looking for your sweater."

"I can buy another sweater," he says.

"Tell that to Grandma," I say.

He sighs. "She made me that sweater. She'll turn the whole hospital upside down until they find it."

"So you answered your own question," my mom says. She strokes his hand like you'd stroke a wounded animal. He *is* a wounded animal. There are purple bruises on his arms where the IVs had been.

"I hope they have better food at this place you're taking me to," he says.

"If they don't," my mom tells him, "we'll bring you food from home."

"You can bring me my stove from home, and I'll cook myself. The rest of you are hopeless."

My mother's eyes fill with tears. Because she isn't hopeless, I guess. The hope is what keeps her going. And maybe what kills her.

"I love you, Mom," I say.

She's startled. "I love you, too."

Grandma Emmy and Madge walk back into the room empty-handed.

"No luck?" my mom asks.

"No," says Grandma. "I hate this place."

"You said it," Grandpa adds. "Can we go now?"

"The nurse will be in soon."

"Where have I heard that before?" says Grandpa Joe, but as soon as he says it, the nurse with the eighties hair and the gun-toting husband shows up with a wheelchair.

"Are we ready?" she says.

"I was ready a month ago," says Grandpa Joe.

Mom and the nurse help Grandpa Joe into the wheelchair. I grab his bag.

"Tola," my mom says. "Check the closets and drawers one last time, okay? I don't want to leave anything else behind."

I check the closets and then the drawers. Behind the curtain, Grandpa's roommate coughs.

I peek around the curtain. He's sitting up, too, his broken ankles propped up in strange casts that look like space boots. And he's wearing my grandpa's sweater. I'm about to say so when he sees me.

"Babydoll?" he whispers.

Maybe he needs the sweater more than we do.

"Good-bye," I say. "Stay warm."

After we get Grandpa settled at the rehab center, I tell my Mom that the school wants to have a meeting early Monday morning.

"Is this about Mr. Mymer?"

"I think so," I say.

Now that Grandpa seems to be doing a little better, she's ready to kick some ass. Mr. Doctor drives. Madge tags along. Grandma Emmy does, too, because she's getting bored at home all alone.

On the way to school, Mr. Doctor thumps his palms against the wheel and the vents blast warm air. My sister jams to her iPod, and Mom and Grandma zone out. It's snowing, the light kind with the big, fat flakes that land softly on the windshield. I open one of the windows all the way. I lean outside and catch the snowflakes on my tongue.

"Tola! It's bloody cold, you idiot!" says Madge.

Mr. Doctor just laughs.

My family files into the school, stamping the snow from our feet. I lead them around the corner to the principal's wing. The principal is waiting outside his office with the school psychologist and a few teachers, staring at the newly painted wall.

"Wow," says Madge, stopping to gape.

"Did you paint that?" says Grandma Emmy.

"Huh," says Mr. Doctor.

"Let me guess," says my mom. "You weren't at June's. And you didn't go to any college seminars over the weekend."

"Mrs. Riley," the principal says. "Can I talk to you for a second?"

A few minutes later, my dad and Hannalore make their way down the hallway, glancing at the crowd of us in confusion.

My dad has a new haircut that makes him look like some over-gelled reality show host. Hannalore has lost some weight on her black rice and fish diet, but not in a good way. It's made her pale and hunched and raw-boned, like an underfed polar bear.

"*Dick,*" says my mom. (To be fair, it is his name.)

"Anita," says my dad.

Mom turns to Hannalore. "Hello, Hanna."

"Hanna*lore,*" says Hannalore.

"Right," says Mom.

"Hi, honey." Dad hugs me with his free arm. Hannalore puts her large head near my face, massages the air with pinched red lips, and then smoothes her white-blond updo as if the effort to be affectionate was too much for her hairpins.

"We're here for the meeting," my dad says.

"What meeting?" sings Madge. "There is no meeting."

"There's no meeting?" Dad says.

Hannalore points at the painting on the wall, sighing in annoyance. "But I think there's a showing."

On the wall, I'd painted a mural in a bunch of different panels:

   1. *Rapunzel Gets a Cat*

   2. *Prince Charming Is a Brown Dude*

   3. *The Evil Queen Weeps*

   4. *Beauty Sleeps*

   5. *The Robber Bride Butchers the Devil*

6. *The False Princess and the Barrel Full of Nails* (or, *Chelsea
   P. Answers Her Own Question*)

A cat dashes between each panel. The border is a chain
of clasped hands.

I painted it way too fast. The proportions are off. The
colors are off. Not everyone will get it. Most people won't.
And that's okay. The most important story you can tell is the
one you tell yourself.

June and Seven come a few minutes later. So do Pete
Santorini, Ben Grossman, and Alex Nobody-Can-
Pronounce-His-Last-Name.

"Tola!" June shouts, and runs over to me. Her cheeks are
round circles of red, her pupils black and dilated.

"Why are you shouting?"

"I'm not shouting!"

Behind her, Seven jerks his head toward Alex Nobody-
Can-Pronounce-His-Last-Name. I don't understand. He
jerks his head again, raising his eyebrows.

And then I get it. June and Alex Nobody-Can-Pronounce-
His-Last-Name? Is this even possible?

"What is going on with you?" I whisper.

"What do you mean?"

I lean in and whisper, *"Alex Nobody-Can-Pronounce-His-
Last-Name?"*

June gets even redder and drops her head. "My phone kept
calling his phone. That's got to be fate, don't you think?"

I take the NASA phone and toss it in the water fountain.

• • •

Me, my mother, and my father confer with the principal and the psychologist.

"You broke into the school," says the principal, Mr. Zwieback.

"No, I didn't," I say. "There was a game. The door was open. I walked right in."

"We can't leave this mural up," he says.

"I know," I say.

"But we can leave it up for the day, can't we?" says the psychologist. She's wearing yet another flammable suit. She must have a whole closet of them. "I think this is very important for Tola's healing journey."

"We can't have the school hallways used for students' healing journeys," says the principal. "And some of this material is not appropriate."

A voice pipes up behind us: "Are you saying that you're going to censor this student's artwork?"

We turn. A woman points a huge camera at us.

"Who are you?" Mr. Zwieback wants to know.

"I'm Dana Hudson. Reporter for the *North Jersey Ledger*."

"We don't allow reporters on the school premises, Ms. Hudson. You'll have to leave."

"I have a responsibility to report the news," the reporter says.

"I have a responsibility to protect my students," says Mr. Zwieback.

"That's okay," I say. "She can stay."

"Good Lord," says Mr. Zwieback as more and more students wander to the mural just to see what's going on.

For the record:

1. "Hey," says Pete Santorini. "Why does Rapunzel get a cat?"

Ben Grossman sneers. "She's trapped in a tower, stupid. It's not like she can get a dog."

"Yeah," says Alex Nobody-Can-Pronounce-His-Last-Name. "Where would she walk it?"

2. Seven stands back from the exhibit, admiring, grinning. "I already have my favorite picked out."

"I bet you do," I say. I painted Seven as I saw him in my jock-punched dreams, bronze skin, silver eyes, crown winking with jewels.

3. Dressed in her finery, a queen fills a porcelain tub with her tears. "Well," my mom says dryly. "The evil queen seems to bear a remarkable resemblance to the artist's mother. Everybody, be sure to get a shot of that one."

Hannalore laughs.

My mother says, "You laugh now. Just wait until you have a couple princesses of your own."

4. Grandma Emmy stares at *Beauty Sleeps* for a long time. In it, an old grandpa dozes peacefully on a bed of rose petals. We stand together, her hand resting light as a kiss on the back of my neck.

5. Madge is transfixed by *The Robber Bride Butchers*

the Devil. It's Madge, in the middle of a dark
wood, with an ax slung casually over her shoulder.
In front of her, a horned man in a vaguely German
military uniform kneels with his head on a stump,
waiting for the bite of the blade.

6. "What is that supposed to be?" says Chelsea
   Patrick, stabbing a finger at *The False Princess and
   the Barrel Full of Nails* (or, *Chelsea P. Answers Her
   Own Question*).

I could tell her the story, but I don't feel like it. Art should
stand on its own without any explanation, right? And I think
the message is clear.

I've painted a barrel lying on its side. Chelsea's body spills
from it, bloodied from the nails visible on the inside of the
barrel.

"It's just a little project I've been working on," I say. "It's
based on a fairy tale. I hope you don't mind."

"What the hell does it mean?"

I give her a hint: "It means you are your own punishment."

I could have tried it her way. I could have made up a website, pretending to be her, saying the most terrible things I
could think of. I could have followed her around, filming her,
and then doctored the footage any way I wanted. I could have
spent a lot of time learning computer programs and technol-
ogy to hide what I was doing.

But that's not me.

I watch as she stares at the image, unconsciously wrapping her arms around herself. I wonder how it feels to be this exposed. I wonder if it feels different to be painted rather than to be videotaped, if there's something worse about someone drawing your bloody naked body stroke by stroke—every bump, every curve, every mark—and then nailing you in the heart.

"They'll just paint over it," she says. "It won't last."

"True," I say. "But it's here now."

"You bitch."

Maybe to her, she's the hero and I'm the villain. And maybe in someone else's tale, I'm nothing but the village idiot. I don't care. Let them paint their own murals.

"You can always call the school board and complain. I think you have their number. And you know what? I gave them yours."

The reporter taps Chelsea on the arm. "Excuse me. Can I get a picture of you with your portrait?"

"Well," my dad says. "This is really something, isn't it?" He searches for something positive to say, which he finds difficult to do when he's not talking about his fabulous new life with Hannalore. "Your technique has improved," he says finally. "And I see you're still obsessed with *Grimm's*."

"Fits my worldview," I say.

"You're too young to have a worldview," says Hannalore.

"We're both very proud," my dad says, wrapping his arm around her waist and squeezing her a little too tightly to be comfortable. "And we're *thrilled* to be here, aren't we?"

"Sure we are," says Hannalore.

The reporter puts me next to Mr. Zwieback and snaps some pictures. I lose interest as Mr. Zwieback is giving a statement, something about my strength in the face of such daunting adversity, how the school is behind me one hundred percent, etc. etc. etc.

Seven says, "The school is behind you one hundred percent."

"Yeah. Behind me. All the better to kick me," I say.

Speaking of kicking, I'm afraid to ask, but I can't help myself. Starving polar bear or not, wicked stepmother or not, Hannalore does own a gallery.

"What do you think?" I say.

She makes a so-so motion with her large, bony hand. "Melodramatic, but that's what you'd expect from a teenager," she says. "Autobiographical, another thing you'd expect." She scans the mural. "None of the panels have your father in them."

"Caught that, huh?"

She smirks. "The words are distracting."

Seven says, "I think the words are the best part."

Hannalore ignores him. "At best, it's juvenilia. At worst, crap."

"Juve–what?" June says.

"You're very kind," I say.

"You asked," she says, unconcerned. I suppose she thinks it serves me right for dragging her out here to this godforsaken suburb when she could be dining on black rice with important people in Manhattan.

I say, "Well, if you can't please everyone with your deeds and your art, please a few. To please many is bad."

Hannalore frowns. A note hits her in the forehead and drops to the floor. She bends at the knees to retrieve it, the perfect lady. The writing is large enough for me to read:

SHOW US YOUR BOOBS!

She holds up the note. "Which of you appalling children threw this at me?"

Pete Santorini, Ben Grossman, and Alex Nobody-Can-Pronounce-His-Last-Name laugh so hard that Alex chokes on his gum and Ben has to pound his back.

Seven pulls me over to the front door, away from the crowds of people. He's brought more cupcakes for me, vanilla cupcakes with mocha icing and chocolate cupcakes with cream cheese icing.

"We don't have much time," I say. "If I'm gone too long, my parents will look for me."

"Then we better make the most of it," he says. He takes a cupcake with mocha icing and smears it across my face. "Uh-oh. Now you're brown."

I take a cupcake with cream cheese icing and slather it on his lips and cheeks. "And now you're white."

He licks his lips. "Tastes good."

"Same here."

"You're just saying that," he tells me. "It's only the second time I've tried the recipe. I changed up the proportions."

"No, it's really good. I've never tasted anything like it. But if you don't believe me, you can check yourself."

He takes a step toward me—all six foot plus of cream-cheese-icing-slathered goodness—and kisses me. It's a sweet kiss, not just because of the icing, but because it's so light, so gentle, like he's kissing me but asking my permission at the same time, *is this okay, do you like this, do you like* me? *Yes*, I think, *yes*. We kiss some more, not as nice, not as sweetly, until the icing on our faces mixes into the most delicious shade of topaz.

I've got a huge crowd now—teachers, students, even Ms. Esme. They pace back and forth in front of the mural, whispering to one another. Sometimes they glance at me and whisper some more.

They're trying to decide if I'm crazy.

They're trying to decide if my art is any good.

They're trying to decide if seeing Chelsea Patrick naked is too horrible a punishment for the public.

They're trying to decide if they believe in fairy tales.

And I want to say, listen, there's no living happily ever

after, just living happily, with the happily part relative, defined by what's possible in the moment. And there's a story here, one familiar and not, where a girl is freed from a tower, a sister is freed from herself, and they go to visit their grandpa. But instead of packing bread and wine, they bring him some ginger ale and maybe applesauce. And the wolves they meet along the way are soft and playful as puppies, the wicked women sing lullabies to their own reflections in their mirrors, and the huntsmen all put down their axes to chase the squirrels through the woods.

Grandma Emmy is peering up at Hannalore exactly the way you'd peer up at an underfed polar bear. Warily.

"How's Joe?" my dad asks Grandma Emmy.

"We moved him to rehab," Madge says. "He ate a piece of turkey and some peaches for lunch. And he walked from the bed to the bathroom by himself."

"That's not enough." Grandma Emmy is still focused on Dad. "You should visit him in the hospital. He likes visitors. People make him feel like eating. Take your girlfriend, too."

"We were married in October."

"Whatever," says Grandma. "Let's go."

"Where?"

"To visit Joe, what do you think?"

"All of us?" my dad squeaks.

"Yeah," says Grandma.

"Now?"

"No time like the present." Grandma points to Mr. Doctor. "But he's driving."

And that's how we all ended up piled in Grandpa Joe's room in the rehab center on a Monday morning, watching a very nice nurse ply him with strawberry Jell-O and crackers. Grandpa Joe is thrilled to see us. Madge is delighted. My dad and my mom look like their underwear is too tight. Hannalore appears to be contemplating gnawing off her own limbs. Mr. Doctor offers to get everyone ginger ale from the soda machine. The nurse tells us all that they hope to get Grandpa back on his feet in a few weeks.

"That's good news," says my mom. She clutches her heart as she speaks, and Grandma Emmy pats her arm.

"Grandpa," I say, moving to the side of the bed. "I have something for you."

"You do?" he says. His voice is weak but not as weak as it was. "Is it something dramatic?"

"Way dramatic," I say.

"And unusual?"

"Take a look for yourself," I say, and pull a small wrapped canvas from my backpack. I help him rip the paper.

It is a brand-new piece. Not one I rushed, but one I've been working on for a while. *Cenerentola Buys New Shoes.* Cenerentola's in a shoe shop surrounded by piles of high heels and sneakers and clogs. Empty boxes litter the chairs and the floor.

But she's trying on a special pair, a pair made just for her.
Glass slippers pronged just like bird's claws.

Well.

If the shoe fits.

Grandpa beams. "That's mighty unusual, Tola. Mighty unusual."

"Yeah, okay," says Madge. "We get it. She's an artistic genius. But on to more important stuff. I'm starving. Anyone up for a trip to the cafeteria? Tola?"

And before I can answer, it occurs to me that, for the first time in a long long time, I feel full.

(comments)

It looks like no one's posted on "my" blog for a while. Not surprising considering I've now got competition like TheTruthAboutChelseaPatrick.blogspot.com and that prom video they can't even put on the ten o'clock news without getting fined by the FCC. But if there's anyone out there still reading this, I thought you might want to know that some reporter is actually writing a book about my story. Or what people think is my story. This is from the press release, which some helpful neighbor shoved into our mailbox:

"The book will concern the scandal that rocked Willow Park High School, leaving a teacher jobless, a teenage girl bullied and devastated, and a community in shock. The book will use interviews from various sources, including school officials, family, friends, neighbors, and classmates, as well as commentary from the victim herself."

Commentary from the "victim." I think they mean me, but if they were interested in talking to

the real victim, it would be Mr. Mymer. He's the one
who lost his job when the whole world lost its collective mind. After I went to the next school-board
meeting and spilled my guts, I sent him a picture of
the mural I painted at the school (it stayed up for two
whole days). I told him how sorry I was. He didn't
write back. At least, he hasn't yet. I suppose I don't
blame him.

Even though I've been talking to reporters a
lot lately—they're all over this "cyberbullying"
thing, which is funny considering they're like a
decade too late—I admit the book idea is a little
weird. But then so many people have said so many
things about me you could write a million books
and they'd all be different. What do I care? Will this
book really be about me? Or will it be about what
other people have decided I am? Am I really "talking" to you now, or is this just some other random
idiot killing time before their favorite show is on? Is
what they say about Chelsea Patrick true, or is she
just another "victim"? Prom video: the unvarnished
truth or someone's nasty home experiment with
Photoshop and iMovie?

I guess it's like everything else.

You have to figure out what you believe all for
yourself.

ACKNOWLEDGMENTS

I started this novel more than a decade ago, so I owe a huge debt of gratitude to a ridiculous number of people. Thanks to Ellen Levine, über-agent, and to Clare Hutton, editor and friend. To Catherine Onder, for her patience, her good humor, and the near-heroic effort that went into the editing of this book, and to Amy Ryan and Ray Shappell for their equally heroic efforts with the design. To Gretchen Moran Laskas, Anne Ursu, Audrey Glassman Vernick, Rosemary Graham, Gina Frangello, Cecelia Downs, Karen Halvorsen Shreck, Zoe Zolbrod, Tanya Lee Stone, Esme Raji Codell, Carolyn Crimi, Esther Hershenhorn, Myra Sanderman, and Franny Billingsley for reading early (and middle and endless) drafts, giving advice, and/or providing snacks. To Cynthia Leitich Smith, Greg Leitich Smith, Katie Davis, Sharon Darrow, Gail Giles, Kathi Appelt, Sean Petrie, and everyone else at the Austin retreat back in June of '04 who read whole or part of the book in one of its infinite incarnations (and made me laugh so much). Thanks, too, to Sheila Kelly Welch and Jessica Metro, who shared their thoughts about making art. To Linda Rasmussen, Annika Cioffi, Tracey George, and Melissa Ruby for . . . oh, you know. And thanks to Steve, always, always, always.